OUT OF CONTROL

LILA ROSE

BLURB

Ryo

He was frustrating, relentless, and determined to believe we had something special. What he didn't realise was that I wasn't like anyone he'd been with before. I was cold, harder, and not worth getting close to. I'd tried to keep my distance, certain that eventually he would see it for himself.

Link

Ryo didn't know it yet, but I was going to be the love of his life. I was prepared to put in the effort to win him over. His aloofness and controlled exterior didn't deter me—I understood they're walls, and I was willing to break through them to prove we were meant to find our way to each other.

AUTHOR'S NOTE:

This is set after Ruin and Wolf's book where Ryo and Link first met.

➤Snippets from Ruin's book, but this part is from Wolf's POV

Link took a seat at the table; I followed suit. Ryo stood behind me. Even when I offered him a seat, he suitably shook his head. Link hadn't offered his guard a seat, though. The guard whispered something to Link, who nodded, and the guard left the room.

"He's going to make a call." He leaned forward, elbows to the table, hands clasped. "Want to get down to business before we eat?"

"That would be good. Did you get a chance to go over the paperwork I emailed this morning?"

He nodded. "I did."

I waited, leaning back in my seat. We'd already ordered our food at the bar while waiting for the room to be cleared.

Link smirked, his gaze briefly shifting over me to Ryo and back again. On the inside, I was cheering that he looked at my friend. I wanted him to notice Ryo. Upon seeing Link in person, Ryo had reacted in a way I'd never seen from him before... by tripping.

Keep looking at my friend. He needs your attention. Fuck the business. He's worthy of your time.

I couldn't say or do anything, unsure what type of look he gave—if he had been checking Ryo out or sizing him up. The man was difficult to read.

"I'd like to accept the deal, but I want to confirm all rights for the businesses will be in my hands."

"Everything, yes."

Link nodded. "It's a fuckin' large amount of money. Are you sure you want to give it up for some person?"

"You obviously haven't met the right person to be willing to do such a thing for. Though, it's also for my family. You do understand the attention this will bring upon you? Our family has always dealt with rivals wanting to take our business."

Link grinned. "You don't need to worry about that. Most are too scared to deal with me. My reputation speaks for itself." I had heard he killed without any remorse, and he was also intimidating to others because the number of men he had on his payroll was vast.

Hmm, maybe Ryo should look elsewhere for someone. I wouldn't want Ryo to be caught in any trouble being associated with Link. Then again, Ryo would call me stupid for underestimating him.

Voices rose outside the door. Ryo gripped my hand, pulled me from my seat, and planted me in front of the table while he then reached over and yanked Link out of his seat, pulling him to stand beside me. Ryo took up position in front of us, gun raised, pointed at the door.

Link's eyes glowed with humour. "Did he just manhandle me to protect me?"

I grinned, my own gun in hand, ready to see what was going on outside the door. "He did."

"Huh," Link grunted and stared at the back of Ryo.

"Sir, you can't go in there" we all heard.

"Like fuck" was snarled by a voice I recognised. "Move."

Ryo relaxed, as did I, and both of us put our weapons away. Link looked from one to another and back again before he asked, "What's going on?"

Ryo snorted. "You'll see." He moved to the door and

opened it just as Josh pushed the waiter to the side and stepped through. "It's all right," Ryo told the waiter.

"You," Josh snarled, pointing at Link. "I don't give a fuck if this is some business meetin' I'm fuckin' up. You do not touch him." His finger shot to me. "He's mine."

My heart danced around in my chest, as did my stomach. Any other time I would be pissed, but since Link was Link, I didn't care.

Link turned to me. "You're fuckin' a Hawks member?" He laughed. "Shit, this is epic. No wonder he stormed in here, ready to kill me. Those fuckers are possessive."

The fight deflated out of Josh, and confusion dipped his brows. "You know Hawks?"

Sighing, I went to Josh and curled an arm around his waist. "Josh, this is Link. He's Travis's old business partner."

Josh huffed. "No shit."

Link held out his hand. "No shit. Whose son are you?"

Josh shook his hand and replied, "Stoke's."

Link nodded. "Met him at Travis and Vi's wedding. Think highly of the Hawks."

Josh grinned. "Good to hear." He rubbed at the back of his neck. "Ah, sorry about before."

"Nah, man, I get it. Not sure how you thought I was coming onto your man, though."

Heat hit Josh's cheeks. "Saw you two at the bar. My mind started overreacting."

Link snorted. "Heard it happens a lot with you guys when it comes to your better halves."

Josh chuckled. "Guess you could say that." Josh glanced at me. "Not sure what business matter you guys are talkin' about, but can you excuse us for a moment?"

Link chuckled and waved a hand. "Go for it."

Josh and I walked back into the room. Josh, of course, placed his hand on my arse on the way. Link thought it was hilarious, especially when he pointed out the hickey while Ryo rolled his eyes, but his lips twitched.

As we sat, Josh suddenly asked Link, "You gay?"

"Nah, mate. Just bi."

Josh grunted. "Know you know this guy's mine." He thumbed my way while I slapped a hand to my forehead. "But Ryo's up for grabs."

The room quieted. I glanced to Ryo and found him blushing and glaring at the ground.

"That so?" Link said.

"Yep."

"Thanks for the information."

CHAPTER ONE

RYO

My gaze narrowed down on my phone when it vibrated again. I always had it on silent because my job was to be seen, not heard, unless my boss, Taro-sama Takahashi, needed me. On the streets, my employer was also known as Wolf, which was what I preferred to use too.

Though, when it came to my job with Wolf, he believed I wasn't needed as much as I had been since he'd cut back on business.

But I could work for Wolf for the rest of my life if I wished.

Not many knew of how I'd come to work for him. Our families had run in the same circles back in Japan, and we'd been lifelong friends, not that our fathers knew. It was best to keep any friendship away from their prying eyes, so they didn't have anything to hold over us.

Which came in handy when I turned eighteen and my family sold me to the Takahashi family. Wolf's father ordered me to become Wolf's personal guard. His life before mine was always rule number one.

Still, I loved my job as his personal guard and assistant.

Wolf had given me a purpose in life and freedom in ways I never would have had with my own family.

Which was why he would always have my loyalty.

Picking up my bowl, I finished my soup for lunch and scowled at my phone again when it vibrated once more.

It had been doing that all morning for the sixth day in a row, and I knew who was to blame for it.

Sighing, I put the dish down and grabbed my phone. I may as well get this over with.

LINK:

Morning, beautiful.

Rolling my eyes, I shook my head. No one had dared call me beautiful.

LINK:

A new day and a new round of
messages for the man I'm gonna marry.

LINK:

Maybe today you'll tell me what I've
done for you to ignore me?

LINK:

I'll buy you flowers, chocolates, a car, a
house. Just tell me.

Ever since the meeting Wolf had with this man where my boss decided to relinquish a large percentage of his seedier businesses to become a silent partner with Link Graham, the man had been nothing but annoying.

Well, to me mainly.

I had thought he was attractive, covered in all that ink and without-a-care attitude.

Until he'd somehow gotten my number and decided to hound me.

LINK:

Dinner? Tonight? Pretty please.

LINK:

I'll make it worth your while.

I wasn't sure why he'd taken such an interest in me,

but I'd already been told that he had many bed partners that could help him with that itch he wanted scratched.

LINK:

> Just take a chance on me, and I bet you'll forgive me for whatever I did as you fall for me.

LINK:

> You've ignored me for nearly a week, but I see you reading my messages. You like me a little bit at least. Let's have that "little bit" grow into something bigger.

LINK:

> Did I tell you how hot you looked standing guard that night? H.O.T!!!!

This man was going to drive me insane. I needed to shut this down, since I would not be seeing him outside of any business-related deals. I worked for Wolf. I did not mix business with pleasure.

Besides, Link would grow bored eventually and go back to one of his conquests.

RYO:

> Please cease the messages. They are unwanted. I refuse all invites. Please find another to annoy.

There, that was clear to understand. Surely, he would do as I asked.

LINK:

> BABY! Hello, my snookums. I miss your stern face, and I only got to see it the once. I need more manhandling, please.

He was an idiot.

I knew he was speaking of when I thought there was danger coming toward the private room we'd been in at the restaurant, but it had only been Ruin showing up at the meeting. I'd pulled both Link and Wolf behind me.

In other words, I'd been doing my job.

LINK:

> What are you doing right now?

RYO:

Ignoring you again. Goodbye.

I stood from the table and took my bowl to the sink. My phone vibrated. I cursed under my breath and gripped the counter.

"How was lunch?" Wolf asked as he and his lover, Ruin, entered.

"Pleasant enough." I faced them and nodded to the guard that I would take over. He disappeared elsewhere. "Tell me once more. Did you or did you not give Link my phone number?"

That stupid device vibrated again, and we all stared at it.

Wolf smirked. "I did not."

A couple of kitchenhands fluttered into the kitchen and got busy making them lunch as they sat at the table.

"You know, I could really get used to being spoilt," Ruin commented as he watched them.

I deadpanned, "Nice to know." Usually, I liked Ruin. He had made my friend happy and was able to show my boss that work wasn't everything in life. However, I'd already been riled, and I wanted answers.

"If not you, then who?" I asked.

There was another vibration, and Wolf went to pick it up.

"Touch it, Wolf, and I'll move in the rest of your family." I could only speak to him in such a way since we were longtime friends. Plus, he ignored my tone all the time, anyway.

Wolf paused, glared, then sat back from my mobile. "Is it so bad that he's contacting you?"

"Yes."

"I saw the way you both looked at each other. The way you protected him when you thought there was danger—"

"I am danger," Ruin put in.

Wolf reached over and patted his hand. "Yes, pet, very dangerous."

He winked.

"I was just doing my job," I informed him again.

Wolf studied me. It was never good when he did, and his next words would prove that. "What did you find out about Link that has poisoned your attraction?"

Wolf and I spent too much time together.

"Nothing."

Ruin coughed into his hand, "Liar."

I scowled at him, but he was too busy watching the food being placed on the table.

"Thank you. Leave us," Wolf ordered. The kitchen staff bowed and fled.

There went my phone again.

I ground my teeth together when my phone screen lit up once more.

"If you don't tell me, I will ask Link what it could possibly be," Wolf warned.

"Do you want me to quit?"

We stared each other down. Wolf's lips twitched. He knew I was bluffing. I would never leave my position.

Sighing, I told him, "I'm not interested in a man who already has many partners. I would prefer to find someone who is looking for a serious relationship."

Ruin asked around a bite of food, "How do you know he's not serious?"

"I…. Well, he couldn't be if he already has so many bed partners."

"And how did you find that out?" Ruin asked after he swallowed.

Clenching my jaw, I looked away. "Someone told me."

"Who?" Wolf demanded.

"Yeah, who the hell would say that and when?" Ruin asked. "I wouldn't've given him your number if he wasn't keen and…. Shit."

"You," I snarled.

"He did it for your own good," Wolf said, sipping his drink.

"You knew?" I demanded.

Wolf rolled his eyes. "Calm down. We only did this because we saw the sexual tension between you both. I knew you wouldn't have made a move on him. When Josh told me Link wanted your number, I told him to give it."

"Maybe he just hasn't found the right person to make an effort for," Ruin suggested.

"Which is ridiculous at his age," I said. He was nearly a decade older than me.

But still very fit and good-looking.

Not that it mattered.

"I would much prefer you tell me who spoke about Link like that. Do you think Link would appreciate being talked about by one of his people?" Wolf asked.

My gaze flared. No, he wouldn't, just like Wolf wouldn't, but Link and his employees weren't my problem, since I wasn't going to involve myself in his life.

"So, it *was* one of his people," Wolf commented.

"Was it that female guard you were talking to at the end of the night?"

Damn him.

"She did look pissed with the way Link was lookin' at Ryo," Ruin said before taking another bite.

Wolf dabbed at his mouth with his napkin. "I agree. What did she say, Ryo?"

"Wolf—"

"Ryo."

"*Taro-sama*, I believe this doesn't involve you."

Ruin snorted while Wolf smirked as he leaned back in his seat. "You are my friend. It involves me."

"This is a private matter. I—"

"It involves me," Wolf stated.

Sighing, I pinched the bridge of my nose. "Fine. Yes, it was the guard who said something, and I won't be telling Link this information. I won't be a part of his life because I refuse to be just another someone in his bed. *I* want to come first, and he won't be able to give that to me. Can we please drop this?"

"What did she say exactly?" Wolf asked, and I knew the stubborn man would not let this drop until he knew.

"She informed me that he has two girlfriends and a few boyfriends already. Herself included. They all know of one another and are willing to share. She asked me if I wanted to join her and him in their bed. I declined. End of story. Now we're leaving this alone. Correct?"

"Fine," Wolf said and resumed eating after sharing a look with Ruin.

A look I did not like.

"Ruin—"

The inked biker suddenly stood. "Shit, I forgot to call my sister back. She's gonna be pissed." He bent, kissed Wolf, and added, "I'll find you after, but then I gotta hit the compound."

"All right, pet."

I would never work out how anyone would be happy and get that dopey look in their eyes over a nickname of *pet*, yet there was proof right in front of me as Ruin melted and kissed Wolf again before leaving.

"Wolf, tell me he isn't going off to call Link."

"Okay," he replied.

"Okay he isn't, or okay you won't tell me he is?"

He quirked a brow. "I'm confused."

"I don't believe you should be. If you can run numerous businesses, you know exactly what I said and meant. Do I need to go and find him to stop him?"

"Then I would be unguarded, and anything could happen to me."

I narrowed my gaze at him. "You're getting on my last nerve."

He grinned. We stared at each other for a moment, all while Wolf ate. That was until my phone vibrated.

"It's a call," Wolf said after glancing down.

Walking over to the table, I saw the name on the screen. "I'll be having a word with *your* lover."

The call from Link ended, just to start up again. I ground my teeth together.

Wolf stood. "I'll be in my office."

I pocketed my phone and nodded, waiting for him to leave, knowing a guard outside of the kitchens would pick up my job if I wasn't at Wolf's side.

"Are you just going to ignore him?" Wolf asked.

"I'm good at ignoring many things." *Like how I want to murder you and Ruin.*

Wolf's phone shrilled. He pulled it out and answered, "Yes? … Correct. … I'll make sure he's available. … Yes." He held it out to me. I glowered. If I didn't take it, I would look like a sullen child.

Snatching it out of his hand, I placed it to my ear. "Ryo."

"Go out to dinner with me and listen to my side, *please.*"

"I have plans," I told Link while glaring at Wolf.

"Wolf told me you're available. Don't you think it's a little unfair that you've judged me from what one person said? Give me half an hour, Ryo."

Sighing, I dropped my head back and stared at the high ceiling. "Half an hour."

"Yes! Same place we met. Six. See you there, snookums," he said and hung up before I could tell him not to call me that.

I handed Wolf's phone back to him, even though I wanted to throw it at the wall.

"You'll be heading out later?" he asked, knowing full well I would be.

"It seems. Have I told you lately that I hate you?"

"First and foremost, you are my friend over your position here. I want to see you happy, and I believe that man can help toward it."

"And if he doesn't? If this is the worst choice?"

"If he hurts you, I'll kill him."

I believed those words. So, I was shocked that Wolf truly thought Link could be the one man for me. Well, he may be for me, but would I be the only one for him?

CHAPTER TWO

Rounding my desk, I again asked my guard, Bradshaw, "Is Cassandra back yet?"

He looked up from his tablet screen. "She's just walked in the front door. Want me to grab her?" When I nodded, Bradshaw slipped out of my office that was on the top floor of the building I owned. This was where I held my computer coding business, but it was also where I handled my other illegal dealings from.

It was lucky I had a bathroom connected to my office and spare clothes because I wouldn't make it home in time to shower and change before my date.

Not that Ryo would call it a date.

Smiling, I glanced at my watch. Soon I would have that feisty man in front of me so I could tell him how she'd been lying. I have slept with people, but I'd never tied myself down.

I'd never wanted to.

Until I saw Ryo standing stonily at Wolf's back.

He was stunningly delicious, and I wanted a bite before I fucking devoured him.

When the door opened, Cassandra walked in with a sultry smile as Bradshaw followed behind her.

Resting my arse against my desk, I crossed my arms over my chest. "Tell me why you think you're allowed to speak to anyone about me and my sex life?"

Cassandra stilled, the smile falling away. She glanced behind her at Bradshaw, who'd closed the door and leaned against it.

"I-I don't know what—"

"Cut the crap. Why did you tell Ryo I'm with many people and ask him to join you and I in bed?"

Instantly, her features morphed from fearful to annoyed before she snapped, "Maybe you'd pay me more attention if I brought him in. I saw the way you *drooled* over that man."

"That man?"

"An Asian? Really, Link? I never thought they'd be your type."

Shaking my head, I smirked. *What a dumb, racist bitch.* "You don't know me, and you never will. You're fired."

"You can't—"

Straightening, I snarled, "I fuckin' can and I fuckin'

will. Shut your goddamn mouth before I staple it closed. Leave, and if I ever find out you've violated your NDA, I'll take your life."

"But—"

"Leave," I roared.

Bradshaw grabbed her arm and yanked her back. He opened the door and led her out.

Fucking bitch. I knew I shouldn't have slept with her, but I'd been lonely that night, and she'd been willing and available.

It seemed my choice had bitten me on the arse and nearly lost me the chance to get to know Ryo more.

It'd been decades since anyone had caught my interest at first sight. Hell, I couldn't even remember the last time that happened.

Not that it mattered right now, anyway, I needed to get moving.

For my date.

Fuck me, but there was that giddy swell inside me like some lovesick schoolboy with his first crush.

Could I possibly get Ryo to kiss me under the make-believe bleachers?

Snorting, I smiled and rolled my eyes. He'd probably cut my head off if I asked.

I'd have to wait and see what type of reception he gave me after hearing what I had to say.

My phone chimed on the way to my bathroom.

TRAVIS:

Good luck, dickhead.

I used to work for the idiot, but he quit the shady shit for his woman, so that left our friendship as the only thing that connected us.

LINK:

Aww, it still touches me, inappropriately, that you care.

TRAVIS:

Fuck off.

Chuckling, I pocketed my phone while thinking and hoping that Ryo would be for me what Vi was for Travis.

Was Ryo going to be special enough to entice me away from all the glorious money I got from trading?

Hell, he could be just as interested in the money and want to run my empire with me.

My cock throbbed at the thought of Ryo guarding and scowling behind me, like he had for Wolf, as I conducted business meetings. Though, I wouldn't want him behind me. I'd try and con him into being under the table, keeping my cock warm in his cute, pouty mouth.

Christ, I was going to have to wank before I left or I'd probably hump his leg.

IN THE RESTAURANT'S private room, I twirled the knife through my fingers and stared at the door, waiting for Ryo to appear. I thought this secluded area would be best, since I wanted all his attention on me and not wandering around a busy restaurant.

Besides, this was where we'd first laid eyes on each other.

It was special.

Like he was.

Okay, maybe I was jumping ahead of myself and allowing my lust to take hold, but fuck me, Ryo was sex on a stick.

The door opened, and a waiter appeared first before moving in and stepping off to the side.

Then… there he stood in the doorway with a scowl.

I grinned as my heart skipped a damn beat.

This man stole my breath.

Pushing back my chair, I stood. "Thanks for coming, Ryo."

His scowl deepened as he stalked across the floor and pulled out the chair opposite me. "Yes" was all he said as he sat. "Half an hour," he reminded me.

My smile grew, and I nodded. Taking my seat again, I told him, "She lied. I don't have girlfriends or boyfriends. I sleep with people but have never been in a steady relationship. I fucked Cassandra months ago, and when she wanted back in my bed, I refused. She no longer works for me."

"All right," Ryo said.

"All right?" I asked as the waiter approached.

Ryo must have heard him, too, since he didn't say anything else.

"Can I get you drinks?" the waiter asked.

"Whiskey with cola. Ryo?"

"Water, please."

Water? Water wasn't a good sign. It made me think I couldn't get him to stay longer than the set time.

The waiter nodded and disappeared.

"Do you believe me?"

Ryo shrugged. "It doesn't matter if I do or don't. It's your life."

I clenched my jaw. I wanted it to matter to him. *I* wanted to matter.

"It does," I told him softly as I shifted the fork on the table and then kept my gaze there as I went on. "I'm around so many fuckin' people. Some who fear me. Some who want to use me. Many who want something from me, but it's all unimportant shit. I have many in my life, but I haven't *wanted* to know any of them." I lifted my gaze and met his semi-wide one. "The only person I've wanted to get to know, in a damn long time, is you. I haven't slept with anyone in a few weeks, and I won't sleep with anyone else while we get to know each other. *If* you'll give me time to get to know you." I took a breath and watched him swallow.

The waiter walked over with our drinks.

"Are we ready to order?"

The ball was in Ryo's court. Did he want to stay and have dinner with me, which would take more than half an hour?

I cocked a brow as he studied me.

"Steak. Medium. With vegetables."

My body hummed as I grinned wide, which he rolled his eyes at.

"And you, sir?"

"Seafood platter," I said, not taking my gaze from the man who still stared me down. He seemed annoyed, while I was over-the-fucking-moon joyful and hopeful.

The waiter left, and I took a sip of my drink.

"Do you want something else other than water now?"

"No. I don't drink."

"Okay. Do you mind if I do?" I'd throw the whiskey over my shoulder if he had a problem with it.

"It doesn't bother me."

"Cool. Tell me something about you, Ryo."

"I work, sleep, and eat. There is nothing else. I'm not interesting."

I smirked. "If this is you trying to discourage me, it won't work. I'll take all your boring days off when you're not working just to spend time with you."

He sniffed and picked up the napkin to place over his lap. "Wolf takes up most of my time."

"I'm sure now that he's with Ruin, you'll have more time on your hands."

"I am not only his personal guard, but also his assistant. I'm very busy."

"That's okay. We can work around it. When are you free next?"

"In four weeks."

"It might kill me to wait to see you again, but book me in for your time, baby."

"Don't call me that."

"Snookums?"

"That either." Ryo pinched the bridge of his nose as he sighed. It was cute how he did that a lot around me. He dropped his hand. "I'm sure you have many interested parties to fill your time. Don't feel you have to wait for me."

"Is that you saying you don't want to be exclusive? I can't do that, Ryo. When I wanna date someone, I can't stand the thought of anyone else touching them." I picked up my knife to twirl it again. "In fact, the thought really fuckin' pisses me off."

His mouth dropped open before he snapped his lips shut. "You don't even know me. Why are you threatening this imaginary person and worrying about being exclusive already?"

He really did seem puzzled.

Poor guy didn't know I had a major crush on him.

Placing the knife back on the table, I leaned forward. "If you're willing to see if we could be a match, I'd like for neither of us to look at, date, or touch someone else."

Just the thought of someone stroking his smooth skin had my gut burning.

"Are you willing, Ryo?"

"Willing to… what? See each other for dinners like we are now?"

"That and more. I want to cook for you. I want to come to your place. I want to kiss you, hug you, and eventually do all the things with you that could make a baby."

An abrupt laugh left him before choking it back.

I beamed.

He glared and cleared his throat while straightening the sleeves of his jacket. "Yes, well, are you asking me to make a decision now?"

"Maybe by the end of dinner."

He nodded stiffly. He was so uptight. I couldn't wait to see him come undone by my hands.

"Thanks, by the way," I added.

"For what?"

"For staying to eat with me."

He hummed under his breath before he picked up his water and took a sip.

"Do you want a soda instead? Or juice?" I offered.

"No. Thank you."

"I didn't tell you when you arrived, but you look amazing."

Holy shit. There was a blush blooming over his smooth cheeks.

Be still my corrupt heart.

He was starting to fall for me.

Smirking, I asked, "What about me?"

His brows pinched. "What about you?"

"Do I look good enough to eat?" *Because you can eat me for breakfast, lunch, and dinner.* Though, I'd much rather do the eating when it came to Ryo.

Christ, the thought of him losing his composure on my tongue was a punch of desire straight to my cock.

His gaze ran over me slowly, and I had the feeling he was trying to make me uncomfortable, but it didn't work. If anything, his appraisal filled me with smugness.

He really did want me. There was a spark in his eyes. Or he could just want to choke me, which I'd be down for too.

"You look fine."

Chuckling, I winked. "I'll take it."

He rolled his eyes, but I caught the little twitch to his lips.

Yeah, I was worming my way into his heart, and I'd fuck anyone over if they tried to mess this up for me.

Ryo would be mine.

CHAPTER THREE

I should have been stronger. I should have said no, and yet, when we'd finished eating and the time came for my answer, I caved.

Link's smile had dropped when I stood to leave at the end, though. I was sure he'd thought I was leaving without saying anything.

I couldn't bring myself to do that. Not when I'd enjoyed his company. Even when he did most of the talking by asking me silly questions that, apparently, would let him know me on a deeper level.

My phone vibrated, and I sighed. I knew it would be him. He was the only one who contacted me during business hours, unless there was an emergency.

I took my phone out of my pocket.

LINK:

> Thinking of you.

There was an image attached of him winking and grinning like a fool.

My lips twitched, until I thinned them. His charm wasn't going to win me over so soon. He could change his mind about me. Grow bored when he realised I wouldn't be easily swayed into his bed.

His worried gaze from the night before swept through my mind.

"You're leaving?" he asked.

I nodded. "Yes."

He pushed his chair back and straightened. I held my hand up when he started to approach and told him, "I'll consider your terms, but I do not rush anything."

His bright smile had my breath catching. "Got it, snookums." He winked. "Don't you worry, I'll earn each kiss, touch, and more. You'll see how serious I am about you."

I scoffed. "You'll grow tired of the chase."

He chuckled. "No fuckin' way, baby. You'll be worth it, and just know that when I catch you, I'll make sure you won't want to escape."

I sighed and shook my head. "You speak as if you want me around on a long-term basis."

"Forever," he said instantly.

He couldn't be real. Shaking my head once more, I told him, "I'll speak to you soon."

I'd quickly gotten out of there because he'd made my heart react in a way it hadn't before. Yes, I'd had lovers, but none of them wanted to get to know me in the way Link showed he wished to.

RYO:

If you must.

A throat cleared. I blinked back into reality and lifted my gaze from my phone to Wolf, who sat across from me in the vehicle.

"Is that smile for who I think it is?" Wolf asked.

Blanking my expression, I pocketed my cell again. "Tell me again why you agreed to this meeting when you've already given him all the information you need to?"

Wolf grinned. "Deflecting. Very well. Ross doesn't believe I've handed everything over to Link. He refuses to deal with Link until I, in person, tell him I'm done with the drug trade."

"And you're allowing Ross to dictate your actions?"

Wolf's grin turned vindictive. "I wish to make sure he clearly understands I'm out of the business and that me and mine are off limits."

"He threatened Ruin?"

"Not exactly, but it was insinuated."

"Will it be just you and I going in?" I asked.

"Yes. The others will wait outside for the signal."

"The signal?"

Wolf cocked a brow. "When the screaming starts. I placed your wakizashi in the trunk."

That was my favourite blade. *Perfect.*

My pocket vibrated; I would check it later. Now I had business to deal with.

"You wanted me here, and now you stay silent?" Wolf glowered at the man opposite the desk. Ross glanced from me, where I stood at Wolf's back, to Wolf.

"Why didn't you come to me with the deal instead of Link? That stupid fucker already owns enough of everything around here."

A wave of fury washed over me. I placed my hand on the hilt at my waist and squeezed. A need pushed at me to draw my weapon free and slice off his head.

Link wasn't a stupid fucker.

He was smart and trustworthy, or else we wouldn't have deemed him worthy of our time and business.

Wolf's hand shot up near his shoulder, telling me to hold.

"My choices are my own business. I don't have to explain myself to you. If you're wise, you will tread carefully when it comes to working with Link. He won't be as lenient as I was. I allowed your little side business. He won't."

He slammed his hand onto the desk. "I'm not afraid of you or that piece of shit—" His scream echoed around the room.

Wolf looked up at me, and I sheathed my weapon.

"I only took a few fingers."

The door behind us flew open, and Ross's men raced in with guns drawn. They looked at their boss cradling his hand against his chest.

"Kill them," he ordered.

"Don't even fuckin' think about it," a new voice said as a gun cocked.

Link entered the room with three others at his back.

The foolish man beamed over at me. "Baby, that sword move was damn hot."

Shock had me jerking my head back.

He tipped his head to the corner of the room. "We installed cameras last night. Pure luck on my part, or else I would've missed seeing you act in my defence."

I sniffed. "The only reason I acted was because he didn't fear my boss."

He winked. "Uh-huh, sure. It was also luck I'd been on my way for a chat with this fuckface." He turned to Ross and fired. Ross bellowed as blood pooled over his upper arm.

"Guns down," one of Link's men ordered loudly.

Link scowled at Ross and bit out, "I didn't like the way you looked at Ryo."

"Dear God," I muttered.

Wolf snorted.

"And I really don't like your fuckin' attitude, Ross. The way I see it, I can either delete you from my world, or you can continue playing your small role by *my* laws and live to see your family again. What do you say?"

"Your rules," he said, wincing.

Link laughed. "I thought so. The cameras stay. I'll be keeping a closer eye on you and your people. Better be a good boy from now on, or I'll allow my man to cut off more than your fingers."

"I am not your man," I told him with a glare.

"You will be, snook."

Did he not care who was around?

I wasn't sure if I liked that about him or not.

Not. No, I didn't like it because it sent my blood pressure sky-high.

This man spun my world out of control, and I felt my cheeks heating.

I looked to Wolf. "Are we done?"

Wolf nodded and stood. "Also know this, Ross. If you come near me or mine, you will suffer in more ways than you can imagine." Wolf strode toward the door, making Link's men move out of the way.

I followed, but it wasn't until we were outside and I'd removed my weapon to place it back in the trunk that I realised Link was there waiting by the car door.

After Wolf climbed into the vehicle, I shut the door and turned to the bouncing man behind me.

He grinned. "Can I kiss you today?"

"No."

His grin widened. "Are you busy tonight for dinner?"

"Yes."

The window on the car wound down. "Ruin and I are staying in tonight, and I'll have the other guards there. You're free to do what you wish."

I scowled down at Wolf. "I wish to work."

"And I wish for you to cut back your hours. You work too hard," Wolf said.

"We'll speak about that later in the office." Meaning I wished for him to keep his mouth shut, and if he wasn't understanding that from my glare, then we were going to have a problem.

"So," Link drew out, "dinner?"

"No." I gripped the door handle and went to open it, but Wolf hit the lock button. "Wolf," I warned.

"Link, would you like to have dinner tonight with Ryo, Ruin, and me?"

That meddling bastard.

Link clapped, and then I felt his hand brush over my back. "Perfect. See you tonight, baby."

"Don't call me that," I shouted to his retreating form and heard his laughter before he entered the house again.

Wolf pressed the unlock button, and I yanked the door open.

The image of strangling my boss and friend made me smile. Wolf scooted over on the seat.

"Maybe if you had told me what happened between you and Link last night, I wouldn't have intervened."

"I'm asking you as my friend to please stay out of this from now on. I'll see Link when I wish to. I've already told him I wasn't free for four weeks."

Wolf studied me before he nodded once. "You have my word I won't interfere any longer."

Sighing, I relaxed back in the seat. "Thank you."

"But since we're now speaking as friends, will you tell me how last night went? Four weeks, seriously?"

Snorting, I shook my head. "You're too nosey."

"It is a fault of mine."

"I enjoyed dinner with him, and I said I'd consider seeing him exclusively."

Wolf smiled. "You're dating."

"We are not. I said I would consider it."

"He already sees you as his," Wolf pointed out.

"I know," I bit out. "But he doesn't mean it."

"I like this for you, Ryo."

My heart stumbled.

I did like Link's attention, too, but I wouldn't allow all my walls to drop and risk being hurt.

"I'll see how things go."

"He shot Ross for the way he looked at you."

Pinching my nose, I groaned. "Please don't remind me."

"I think it's sweet, since you did cut off Ross's fingers for the words he used against Link."

"I did not."

Wolf smirked. "Sure."

At least I never would admit that I let my anger get a hold of me for that brief moment.

CHAPTER FOUR

LINK

A guy named Katon showed me into the ginormous house. I got a kick out of taking off my shoes and putting slippers on. Made sense, though. Saved the dirt coming off my shoes into the clean place.

I walked into the room Katon had pointed to and muttered, "Holy shit." Ryo looked hot in his suits, but he looked smoking in jeans and a plain black tee. "You look delicious," I told him as I walked up to the huge-arse table.

His cheeks pinked, and he snapped, "Shut up."

Ruin chuckled, and Wolf smiled as he watched his friend.

I took the seat next to Ryo and gazed at the food in front of us.

"It was just placed down when we heard that you'd arrived," Ryo told me.

I winked. "All good, baby."

"Don't call me that."

"You got it, snookums."

Ryo sighed and glowered at Wolf.

"Ruin, good to see you. How's the brothers?"

"Same, same. How's life since the last time I saw you?"

Looking to Ryo, I answered, "Great."

"Let's eat," Ryo said.

We dished up our food while Ruin told us a story about his friend, Texas. I kept glancing over at Ryo. I couldn't get enough of watching him. He moved gracefully even as he ate. I didn't want to look away. Also, he was damn handsome and cute with the way he made a point of ignoring my stare.

"Link, how did things finish with Ross?" Wolf asked, and I realised Ruin had finished talking and that I'd missed most of his story.

"Yeah, fine. We'll keep an eye on him. Ruin, you should've seen my man—"

"I'm not your man."

"—at the meeting. He cut off the guy's fingers because he'd called me a stupid fucker."

Ruin chuckled. "I heard."

"I did not do it for you," Ryo tried to say, but I knew the truth. He so wanted me.

Reaching over, I patted his thigh and felt him tense

under my hand. "It's okay, snook. Like I said, I thought it was hot."

He rolled his eyes and went on eating while I kept my hand on his thigh. I used the other to pick up my fork.

"Have you spoken to Travis lately?" Ruin asked.

"All the time. The guy misses me too much." His fault for staying in Ballarat all the damn time.

Ruin snorted. "Sure, he does."

Ryo placed his hand over mine on his thigh, and I was about to praise the hell out of him, until he picked it up and dropped it on my own thigh.

"You know Travis is only a friend, right?" I asked, worry twisting my gut at the thought I'd upset him with my words.

Jesus. I really had fallen hard into this attraction for the man next to me.

"I know. He's married to Violet, and they have a daughter, Izzy. You also have a sister named Trisha who is married to a man named Henry. They recently had their second child, another son. They live in America because of Henry's work. You prefer your coffee black with one sugar. You have many employees, but the longest running is Bradshaw, who is your personal guard and computer specialist when you can't do the work yourself since you have a computer engineering degree. You also have a degree in business management. I know a lot of things about you, Lincoln Graham."

He'd investigated me.

I mean, of course he had. It would've been stupid if they didn't, for business's sake.

Still, I liked that Ryo knew things about me.

"You'll meet my sister one day."

"No, thank you," he replied, sipping at his water.

"Also, is it inappropriate to let you know I'm hard from all the information you know about me?"

His cheeks pinked, and he very quickly glanced down, then up and away.

Fucking cute.

Ruin guffawed, while Wolf snorted, and my handsome prince glowered at the wall.

"Very inappropriate," Ryo finally said. "And at your age, you should know better."

When he looked back to me, I winked. "You can call me daddy any time you want, snook."

His blush deepened, as did his scowl. But his friends found me amusing.

Leaning into Ryo, I told him, "I may be nine years older than you, snook, but I bet I'll keep up in *any* circumstance."

Ryo suddenly stood. "I need the bathroom." He stalked out of there like his jeans were on fire.

"Did I push too much?" I asked, turning to Wolf and Ruin.

"I don't think so," Ruin said. He looked to Wolf.

"Are you serious about a relationship with Ryo?"

"Yeah," I said to Wolf.

"You had better be, Link. If you screw with him, I

will end our deal and make sure you pay for hurting him."

My skin prickled. I hated threats, but I would take this one, since it was for Ryo's sake. "I get you wanting to protect him. I'd never intentionally hurt him, and I'll do everything I can to make sure I don't. But shit happens. I can't look into the future. Still, you gotta know that I haven't wanted anyone as much as I do him in a long time, and that's only after a few times seeing the guy. I can only image how obsessive I'll become after dating him for a while and he gives me his everything. I won't want to give him up. I'll want to keep him forever. He doesn't know just how possessive I can get."

Wolf smirked. "I think he's gathering it." He sobered and quietly said, "However, you also need to consider that what you're now getting from Ryo in front of others may be all he can offer. He's not used to showing the… softer side around other people. I'm sure he'll be different behind closed doors, but out in the open, he controls himself."

How had he gotten that way?

I wanted to know. I wanted every bit of information I could get on Ryo Sato.

Shrugging, I swallowed my mouthful and said, "I already like Ryo as he is."

Wolf grinned. "I may like you, Link."

Smirking, I cocked a brow. "You're only figuring this out now?"

Ruin clipped. "And he means platonically."

Chuckling, I rolled my eyes. "I get it, Ruin. You've pissed all over Wolf."

Ruin nodded, looking smug.

"All right, so I keep doing what I'm doing when it comes to Ryo?"

Wolf nodded, and his gaze moved over to the doors. I glanced back to watch Ryo approach.

He took a seat beside me again and picked up his fork.

"Missed your face," I told him.

His brows pinched. "Doubtful. I was only gone for a moment."

"Still missed you." I turned back to Wolf. "You gotta fire your cooks so I can hire them. This shit is the best." I sawed into the steak and popped the piece into my mouth, moaning around the meat that melted against my tongue.

Thinking of meat and my mouth, I glanced at Ryo, wanting his meat between my lips. I'd pay it the special attention it needed.

"Stop looking at me," Ryo said with his eyes to his meal.

"I can't help it. I bet you'd be just as delic—" I chuckled around the spring bean he'd shoved in my mouth.

Wolf pushed his chair back and stood. "This has been lovely, but Josh and I are tired—"

"We are?" Ruin asked, the fork with a pile of food on it raised near his mouth.

Wolf threaded his fingers through Ruin's hair and gripped. "Yes, pet. Very tired."

"Right." He faked a yawn as he placed the fork down on his plate. "But if I wake up in the middle of the night, I can get someone to bring me food?"

Wolf nodded. "Of course."

"You're not being subtle at all," Ryo said while glowering at them. He faced me. "Looks like dinner is done. You may go."

Grinning, I shook my head. "Thanks for the offer, but I'm gonna finish this awesome food first. You can stay and keep me company."

His jaw clenched.

"Goodnight," Wolf called, dragging Ruin toward the door.

"Catch ya," Ruin said before we heard him say to Wolf, "We're getting food to the room now, right?"

Wolf sighed just as the door closed after them, so if he said anything in return, I wasn't sure.

While we ate in silence, a couple of waiters came in and took some trays away, and I smirked around my mouthful, knowing that they were getting the food for Ruin.

"Do you have family?" I asked between my last bites.

"Yes" was all he said.

"Cool. Parents? Siblings? Cousins?"

"All of the above, plus aunts and uncles. I have had nothing to do with them since the day my parents sold me, at eighteen, to the Takahashi family to become their loyal servant. They also wanted me to be their spy. It was pure luck I got placed with Wolf. When he gave me the option to cut my family from my life and to become whoever I wanted to be, it earned him my loyalty. That is why I've stayed at his side since."

My gut clenched. I despised that for him. "Shit, Ryo. That fuckin' sucks. But what about your siblings?"

"My two older brothers work for our father and stood beside him when they sold me. My life is better off without any of them in it, and once I informed them that I wouldn't be supplying them with any type of details about the Takahashi family, they dropped me from their lives." He took a gulp of his water. "That was after they tried to have me killed."

"What the fuck?" I blurted. "Serious?"

He grinned. What would he be grinning about?

"All five attempts failed due to Wolf and I stopping them. Then I figured, when no one else tried for years after, that my family refused to pay another person to fail. Besides, they're too lazy to try and kill me themselves."

"Jesus, Ryo. Can I kill them?" Why hadn't he?

He pushed his plate away and shook his head. "I want nothing to do with them and no one else in my life to bother with them either."

My heart skipped a beat.

"Am I in your life, baby?"

He looked away, cheeks tinting again. "No."

He glanced down at the table as I walked my fingers

across the wood to tap the back of his hand before I picked it up in mine and drew it slowly to my mouth, then kissed his fingers.

He swallowed thickly.

"I think I already am, and I'll go at any pace you want to set." I nipped at his knuckle.

He cleared his throat and slowly removed his hand from mine. "We will see."

That we would.

CHAPTER FIVE

RYO

There was a crack in my armour around my heart ever since the night Link had dinner with us, and he was slowly seeping his way in.

But I wouldn't give in to him.

I still believed he would grow bored and find someone else to annoy.

What I didn't like was how the thought of him with another person twisted me up inside.

Which was ridiculous. I should know by now that becoming attached to someone wasn't good. They could wreck your life in ways I didn't have time for.

My focus was work.

Still, Link kept trying to push his way in.

It'd been two weeks since I'd last seen him, but he never stayed quiet.

He called, texted, even emailed to ask me about my day, telling me about his, and then wanting to know more about me.

It was frustrating how charming he was.

Gripping the steering wheel, I thought about turning around and heading home once again.

When my phone rang through the car, I quickly accepted the call.

"Tell me you need me back there," I said to Wolf.

The idiot laughed. "I do not. You already gave me extra guards while you're not here."

"You've been attacked at home before, and until everyone understands that you no longer deal in the gun and drug trade, I will have you protected at all times."

"I know, Ryo. I appreciate the care."

"I don't care."

"It's me you're talking to, friend."

Sighing, I unclenched my hands and took turns shaking each one out. "Sorry."

"Try and let your walls down around Link while you're there."

While I was *there*.

At *his* house.

He'd finally managed to con me into having dinner with him, but he'd only told me at the last moment it would be at his place.

"I'll see."

Wolf snorted. "You have protection with you, yes?"

My heart raced as I spluttered out, "I am not sleeping with him."

I heard Ruin's loud laugh in the background and Wolf's soft one. "I wasn't speaking about sleeping with him. *That* was where your mind went."

I scoffed. "Then what did you mean?"

"Have you taken guards with you? I'm not the only one who needs security. You're a big part of my world, Ryo, and I don't want anything to happen to you."

Softening, I relaxed into my driving. "Two of the men are following me."

"Good. Now have fun at your lover's place—"

"He's not my lover."

"If I don't see you in the morning, I'll know where you'll be."

"I'll be home soon."

"Don't worry about any work here. Just have fun."

"I don't have fun."

Wolf laughed. "You can, though. Just remember that." He ended the call before I could say anything else.

It was probably for the best, since I didn't want to be in a foul mood when I arrived at Link's, and I was already pulling up to his gate.

Although, I had a feeling that if I was in a mood, Link wouldn't care.

Rolling down my window as the guard approached, I tipped my chin and said, "Ryo Sato, here to see Link. I have a vehicle behind me that contains my own securi-ty." The man looked familiar. I was sure he'd been at the restaurant.

The guard grunted. "Hey, name's Bradshaw." Link's personal guard. "Boss sent me out here to let you in. Usually, it's a full scan of ID and car, but he trusts you." His stare told me that I better not go against Link's faith in me if I wanted to live.

I nodded.

"You okay with your guards hanging outside the gate here? You'll be safe within the walls. Boss has the highest security system, and the people in the building have already been screened well. They're loyal to Link."

Did I trust Link with my safety around him and his own?

No.

Yes.

Maybe.

Clenching my teeth, I nodded once again. Bradshaw left to speak to my men.

My skin itched at the thought of placing my trust in someone else.

For many years, the only person I had faith in was Wolf. Even when others had proved themselves safe, I still held them at arm's length.

Sighing, I tightened my grip on the wheel when the gates opened, and then I got a text from one of Wolf's men in the car behind me. I confirmed that Bradshaw was correct with his instructions.

My stomach was a ball of nerves as I parked near the stairs to the front porch. When I climbed out, the front door opened, and my blood pumped harder and faster through my veins when Link stepped out in jeans and a long-sleeved black top.

His smile was sinful, and I watched as his gaze ran over me slowly, spiking the beat of my heart.

"Hey, baby," he called.

"Don't call me that," I told him, walking up the stairs.

"I'll try to remember that, love."

I wanted to pinch the bridge of my nose and sigh, but I just stared at him.

Link chuckled and waved a hand toward the doorway. "Welcome to my home, where I hope you'll spend a lot of time."

Since I noticed he wore no shoes, I stepped into the entryway to remove my own and then waited for Link off to the side as he shut and locked the front door.

"I know it ain't as big as what you're used to—and I'm only talking about the house, not my dick; you can look at that any time you want—but let me show you around."

This man.

I wanted to laugh but also smack the back of his head.

Instead, I nodded and stayed silent. Link pointed to the left and explained that was where the formal dining room was. To the right was his office. Down the end of a small hall, where an amazing smell was coming from, we walked into the family room and kitchen area that had seating at the counter. I also noticed a wok on the stovetop that held something that made my mouth water. He walked by the stunning black-and-white kitchen and through the large pantry to another hallway. Straight across from it was the guest bedroom and bathroom. Down the left end of the hall lay the lounge room. At the opposite end was a movie room. Over at the other side of the house, across from the kitchen and family room, was where the magic happened—his words, not mine—with his big bedroom, walk-in robe, and bathroom. There were also three other bedrooms, a laundry, and another bathroom.

I would admit I'd read Link wrong. I thought his home would be extravagant, over the top, but this felt humble, sweet, and homey.

I liked it a lot—not that I would tell him, though.

When we made our way back into the main area, he asked, "What do you think?"

"I…." I tightened my jaw at the hopeful gleam in his gaze. I hated that it affected me in a way where I suddenly needed to tell him the truth. With a sigh, I said, "It's nice."

He chuckled. "Did that hurt you to say?"

My lips twitched. "Yes."

He swept in and kissed my cheek before dancing back again. "Thanks, snook." He went to the kitchen and grabbed some bowls from the cupboard. "I made veggie dumplings. They're in the steamer, but I've also got miso hoikoro Japanese pork and cabbage stir-fry." He stilled before facing me. "You do like that, right? I should have asked what you like. Shit."

My heart hammered into my ribs.

"You made this?"

"Yeah. I like cooking. Though, I really would employee Wolf's chefs if he wanted to get rid of them."

He'd cooked.

This man who traded in guns, women, and drugs had been at home thinking of me and what I would like for dinner.

Swallowing thickly, I glanced away and said, "I like this dish." It was one of my favourites.

"Awesome. How many dumplings you want on the side?"

"Whatever you give me." I pressed a hand to my swirling stomach and watched him dish me up the food.

His large, tattooed hands were works of art and meant to be admired.

I could admit to myself that I wouldn't mind seeing them glide over my body.

My cock jerked.

I quickly looked elsewhere and clenched my teeth.

"You good to eat in the movie room? We can watch something."

"Not the dining room?" I asked.

He chuckled. "I know you're used to big family

dinners or even small ones and being served at a table, but it'd gonna be a bit different here."

Had I sounded rude? I didn't mean to.

"Movie room is fine."

He glanced over his shoulder and grinned. "Cool. Wanna grab some bottles of water? I'll carry the bowls."

I nodded and went to the refrigerator. Opening it, I noted that there was a whole shelf dedicated to water.

He wouldn't have bought them just for me.

Many other people drank water.

Removing two, I closed the door and turned to see him waiting by the pantry that we'd walked through to get to the movie room. The large, deep bowls were piled high, and I wasn't sure I could eat it all, but I wanted to try.

Damn this man for making me feel something.

I followed him into the movie room and took a seat beside him on the large black couch that I sank into. After placing my water in the cup holder in the armrest, I passed his over and took the bowl Link offered.

He picked up the remote. "What are you in the mood for?"

"Anything." I forked a dumpling and shoved it in my mouth, biting into goodness. My eyes widened, and I glanced down to count how many I had.

"There's more, if you want," Link said. I saw his happy grin as I glanced at him and nodded.

He ended up picking an action movie while we ate in silence.

It surprised me how comfortable I felt alone in a room with Link.

Every now and then, I peeked out the corner of my eyes to watch him laugh or smile at something on the massive screen. He caught me a couple of times and winked before I quickly looked away.

This man was attractive, sweet, and kind—at least to me, so far.

But could it all be an act until he got what he wanted?

It still stunned me that he wanted to sleep with me. I didn't think he'd find me good-looking or interesting. Not when I'd been nothing but cold and short with him since we'd met.

Why was he wanting my time?

Why did he continue this game of chase?

And would it all change when I gave in?

When?

I meant *if* I gave in, not when.

CHAPTER SIX

LINK

Ryo was in my house. His scent filled the room, and yet I still wanted to bury my nose into the crook of his neck and inhale. I was addicted.

Would he get mad if I licked him all over?

Licking meant claiming, and I wanted to claim every fucking inch of his stunning self.

I knew I was getting under his skin.

I knew he liked that I cooked for him.

Cracks were starting to show in his walls, and I couldn't wait until I broke all of them down.

I had a feeling he would only show his true self and let go when he'd given me the gift of being inside him.

Christ, my cock throbbed at the idea of Ryo with his head thrown back while I thrust into his sweet ass. There would be nothing else on his mind but me. I'd make sure of it.

When Ryo finished, I asked, "Do you want some more?"

He looked from his dish to me and back again, almost like he was surprised he ate it all. "Maybe?"

My lips twitched as I held out my hand for the bowl.

"I can get it," he told me, jaw clenching.

"I know, but I want to."

His gaze narrowed on me. "Fine."

With a smirk, I took his dish and made my way into the kitchen.

I liked this already. Him being in my home. Alone with me. All I had to do was get him to stay for the rest of his life, but I knew that'd be something that'd take a lot of work.

He was worth it, though.

All his prickliness was cute.

Not that I'd tell him that. He'd probably try to stab me.

Back in the movie room, I handed him his bowl and sat back down.

"Thank you," he grumbled.

"You're welcome, snook."

He was too busy eating to reply, but he shot me another dark look before focusing back on the screen.

Hell, I couldn't even remember the last time I shared my house and time with someone like this. Yeah, I fucked people, but I never took them to my own bedroom. I'd always used one of the other rooms, and that was sparingly too. I preferred going to their place.

But with Ryo, I wanted him in my room. I wanted him sprawled out on my sheets, waiting for me.

He probably thought I'd grow bored of him, but I knew I wouldn't.

I'd prove it. I'd take it slow like he needed and show him I wasn't walking away before or after he gave in to what was growing between us.

He'd be mine one day.

"What are you smiling at?" he asked, waving his utensil at the screen. "They just beheaded someone."

I turned my head his way, grinning. "You been watching me, love?" I leaned toward him, and he drew back. With a chuckle, I rested on my side again and faced the movie. "I was smiling at the thought that one day you'd be mine."

He coughed and choked over a mouthful. I reached over and patted his back. It would probably be wrong to slip my hand under his shirt to help.

"Shut up," he croaked before taking a gulp of his water.

"Relax, snook. I'm more than willing to wait. No matter how long you hold out."

His jaw clenched as he sniffed. "Then maybe I will give you what you want to finally be rid of you."

Laughter burst out of me. I placed my empty bowl on the floor and shook my head. "Baby, if you think giving yourself to me will bore me in the end, you'd be dead wrong."

He huffed. "You cannot know that."

He didn't know me yet, so he didn't understand that when I fixated on something, I never let it go. And okay, I'd never been this taken by a person, but deep in my bones, I already knew I wouldn't give him up either.

I'd have my damn ring on his finger.

"Snook, I do."

He let out a frustrated groan before he placed his bowl on the floor. "Watch the movie, Link."

"You'll see."

"Watch the movie."

"Babe, what are you afraid of?"

"Nothing," he stated.

"Bull. I have a past, but I wouldn't fool around with someone's feelings if I wasn't serious. If you're attracted to me and agree to give us a chance, I'll do everything in my power to prove that your risk was worth it."

He glowered over at me, crossing his arms over his chest. "Can you honestly say you see yourself with a man for the rest of your life?"

"Yes."

"What about children?"

"We can adopt."

"I work for Wolf. I won't leave—"

"I can move in with you."

"You have an empire to run. An illegal empire that my boss gave a large chunk of up because he wants his family safer than it was."

Shit.

"We'll think of something. Hell, I'll buy the joint next door, and we can build an underground tunnel for you to sneak in and out of so no one from my business will come at you or Wolf." I sat up. "Actually, that's a fuckin' brilliant idea. I don't want you harmed in any damn way, so if we have a tunnel—"

Soft laughter had me shutting the fuck up so I could listen to it. Ryo had his eyes closed as he used the back of his hand to cover his mouth while he shared his mirth with me.

When he opened his eyes and saw me watching, a blush rose, and he snapped his lips closed.

I smiled. "Love" was all I said.

He shook his head. "You're crazy."

"For you, yeah, baby."

"Don't call me that."

"Okay, love."

"Or that. Now watch the movie."

"Can I move closer?" I asked.

He stiffened. "No."

"Just a little." I pinched my thumb and forefinger together.

He sighed, pinching the bridge of his nose for a moment before staring my way. "Will you then shut up?"

"Completely."

"Fine."

"Fuck yes." I grinned and scooted close. In a quick move, I placed my arm around his shoulders and adjusted him to lean against me.

"I did not say you could do this."

But he didn't shift away either. Though, he was as stiff as a board.

Reaching down between us, I lifted his arm enough to rest his hand on my thigh. "Just relax, snook. Enjoy this moment on our third date."

"It's not a date."

Chuckling, I brushed my nose against his temple. Drawing in a breath, I then asked, "Then what would you call it?"

"Acquaintances watching a movie together."

"And you're curled into me for...?"

He tipped his head back, glaring up at me. "That was your doing."

Chuckling, I kissed his nose, which made him quickly look away as his face heated. "Yeah, I know, and I'd do it again." I gently squeezed him against me.

I fucking loved that he was right here.

Ryo sniffed like he was put out, but again, he didn't move. What he did do was slowly unlock his limbs so they weren't struck tight from tension.

About half an hour later, he'd fully relaxed, and his head slipped back as he made a cute, soft noise as slumber took him under.

Holy fuck.

This was big.

It was damn huge.

I never thought he'd be comfortable enough around me to relax like this. Not yet at least.

Of course, I *had* to take my phone out and snap a couple of pictures.

My damn fingers tingled at the urge to send them to Wolf to show him this massive development.

Although, if Ryo found out I did, he'd have my balls.

Not that I wouldn't give them to him freely now.

So instead of sending them off, I placed my phone down and watched the rest of the movie with my exhausted man at my side.

But of course, I didn't pay much attention to the movie. Not when I could keep looking at Ryo. His lips were parted slightly, and I wanted to stick my tongue in there.

Hell, I wanted to lick him all over.

But what I wanted the most was a kiss.

Just a simple kiss that I knew would have my pulse racing.

Just thinking about touching my lips to his had my gut stirring in a good way.

His body jolted, and he sat up, looking around.

He glanced back, face warm. "I fell asleep." He'd said it like he couldn't believe it.

"You did. Must mean you feel comfortable around me."

He glared back. "No."

"Oh, I think it does."

"I don't sleep well. Never have since I was young and beaten awake by my family."

His fucking family.

I wanted to destroy them.

Scooting forward, I slid to my knees and moved on them to stop in front of a wide-eyed Ryo.

"What are you doing?" he demanded.

I shifted in, pushing his legs apart to get close. "Getting to my knees to beg you to let me kill your family."

He froze for a beat, and then the delight he showed me as he laughed once more was something that warmed my corrupt heart.

Christ, he was stunning.

Of course it didn't last long.

He regained composure quickly, thinning his lips, even though they twitched.

Until he sobered completely as he stared at me.

I tried for a charming smile, and his gaze narrowed.

When I winked, his jaw clenched.

"I'm going to kiss you," I told him. I couldn't resist any longer.

To my surprise and elation, which had my pulse racing, he didn't say anything to stop me. I leaned in and brushed my lips over his in a quick kiss before I pulled back and grinned.

"Is that all?" he asked. Then his eyes widened briefly before he went back to scowling. "I should go." When he went to make a move, I gripped the back of his neck, and as I tugged him forward, I leaned in and met his lips again.

A simple few pecks, until he let out a frustrated noise and slanted his mouth over mine, forcing his tongue into my mouth to dance with mine.

Fuck yes, baby.

Grinning around the kiss, I gave as good as he did while we fought with our tongues, teeth, and lips. My cock fattened, wanting his attention.

I groaned when he roughly nipped at my bottom lip.

Christ.

Would this be how he'd go off in bed?

"Jesus, baby," I muttered, trailing my lips down his neck. "Fuckin' love your mouth."

His fingers dug into my waist. "I should go," he said again, but this time it came out soft and husky, making my cock throb.

With a final lick and suck to his neck, I pulled back and nodded. "Probably for the best because I need to jerk off after that kiss."

His face heated before he palmed it and shook his head. He stood, straightening out his clothes. "Goodbye."

Standing, I grinned. "Baby, I can hold off until I walk you to the door. Unless you wanna stay and watch me."

Holy fuck.

Glee saturated my senses when he actually took a moment to think about it.

He wanted to. I could totally tell. What helped was the knowledge that he was as turned on as me, if his erection under his jeans was anything to go by.

He shook his head. "I have to go."

Pinching his chin, I told him, "Loved having time with you, snook."

He glared, and even that made me happy. "Don't call me that," he said, but there wasn't too much heat behind it.

"Can I hold your hand while I walk you out?"

He gaped. "No."

"Next time." I waved him toward the doorway, and he stiffly turned and strode out. At the front, he placed his shoes on and went to open the door, until I reached over his shoulder and pressed my palm against it. "Nah-ah, baby. I need another goodbye kiss."

"You've had enough."

Chuckling, I threaded my free fingers into his hair and yanked.

My blood flooded to my cock when he made a breathy little moan.

I moved in close behind him and mouthed the side of his neck. "Damn, lover, can't wait to hear what other sounds I can bring outta you."

I managed another kiss and suck on his skin before he used his ass to push me back to get the front door open to flee into the night.

"Night, snook," I yelled.

"Don't call me that," he called back before he got into his car and started it.

Goddamn, this was gonna be fun.

That man had me all twisted up in the perfect kinda way where I was ready to lock him away and hide the key.

CHAPTER SEVEN

hy did that fool like me? I was hot and cold—mainly cold—all the time, and yet he still wanted to know when we could see each other again. I'd been ignoring him for a week now, and he wasn't letting up.

Idiot.

That kiss, though.

It had been the best one I'd ever received, which was why this wouldn't work.

I wished he'd just quit trying because then it'd save me from getting hurt.

Not that I'd let him hurt me.

I made a rule the day my family sold me that I wouldn't allow anyone else to hurt me like they had.

Growing up, I used to see happy families around me and wonder what I did wrong to be treated like I was nothing but a pest to them.

Working with Wolf gave me purpose. I found a place I was content in.

But Link was throwing me off balance.

I jolted when my phone vibrated again in my pocket. I set down the gun that I was cleaning but refused to look at my cell even when my hands ached to grab it.

Wolf sighed and looked up from the paperwork on his desk. "Why are you ignoring him?"

"Him who?"

"The man who is completely smitten with you."

I stared blandly at him. "I don't know who you're talking about."

Wolf smirked and cocked a brow. "He's really under your skin."

Glaring, I demanded, "We're dropping this subject."

"You like him."

"Like a hole in the head."

"You want him."

"I want to choke him," I told him through clenched teeth.

He smiled. "I don't need to know about your fetishes."

"I will kill you," I threatened.

He chuckled.

My phone vibrated again, but this was longer. A call.

"Answer it," Wolf said.

Sighing, I pulled out my phone, but the number wasn't one I knew. On answering, I commanded, "Who is this?"

"Bradshaw."

My blood froze.

"There was a situation. Link got shot and—"

I stood, gut twisting. "Where is he? Is he all right? Tell me where he is right now," I demanded, stalking from the office and down the hall with Wolf following.

If anything happened to him….

Pangs of worry stabbed me in the chest.

"We're at the main gate at your boss's place, but since Link is bleeding all over the place, they won't let us in." Why did he sound so calm about it?

"I'll deal with them," I said and hung up. "Link is bleeding out in the car at the gate," I told Wolf while calling the gatehouse.

"Sir?" one of the guards answered.

"Open the gate and let Link in."

"But—"

"Now or I remove your head from your shoulders." I hung up and rushed to the front door. "Can you call for the doctor? I'll get Link to my room."

Wolf nodded. "Of course."

Yanking the door open, I ran down the front stairs just as a black vehicle pulled to a stop. The back door swung open before I got there, and when Link popped out of the car with a smile on his face, I halted.

He had a little bit of blood on his sleeve near his upper arm, but that was it.

"Snookums," he called.

I flicked my gaze to his face and glared. "You were supposed to be shot and bleeding out."

He tipped his chin. "Hey, Wolf." When he glanced back at me, he pointed at the red on his shirt. "I was. It hurts like a bitch. Heard you threatened to cut the guard's head off if I wasn't allowed in." He chuckled. "Love it."

"You were supposed to be bleeding everywhere."

"Well, I did get a bit of blood in the car. Bradshaw may have exaggerated on my behalf a little. They wouldn't let me in because I didn't have permission or an appointment after my ordeal of being shot."

"Wolf," I called while glaring at Link.

"Yes, Ryo?"

"Give me your gun." I'd left my half-cleaned one in his office as I ran out like an imbecile.

"I don't think—"

Link's hands rose in front of him. "Baby, don't be mad. You've been ignoring me, so when Bradshaw and I *were* being shot at, to the degree we could have lost our lives, I knew exactly where I wanted to go. I had to see my buttercup."

"Wolf, gun now."

"Ryo," Link whined, pointing at his arm again. "I'm hurting here. Come pay me attention."

Fury pumped through my veins. My heart was

slowly crawling from my arse up to my chest again after learning Link had been shot and was bleeding out.

I held my hand out to my friend, waiting for the steel to be dropped into my palm.

The front door of the driver side opened, and Bradshaw stepped out. "You're not really gonna shoot him?"

"Yes," I replied, jaw clenching.

"Baby—"

"Don't call me that," I snarled.

I'd been worried.

No, it was more than that. All I could think was that I'd lost my chance to be with him and I wasn't going to get to see him again.

It had crushed me.

Fuck him for making me feel that way.

Fuck. Him.

Turning, I stalked back into the house.

"Snook, wait. Come on," Link called.

I heard footsteps but ignored everything and everyone as I tried to cool the burn in my chest.

"Shit," he bit out.

I'd rushed out of the house like some lovesick fool worried about someone they cared for.

No, I'd acted like I was in a tizzy for someone I was trying not to care for, and all he did was play a trick on me.

"Ryo, wait," Link called when I was halfway up the stairs.

I didn't wait. I just kept on going. It was lucky I

didn't have a weapon on me, or I really did think I would have shot him myself.

I still could.

He deserved it.

I headed for my bedroom where I had many weapons to pick from.

"Hey, Ryo, what's going on?" Ruin asked when he stepped out of one of the gyms.

"Murder," I replied and kept walking.

"Do I need to worry?"

"No." Besides, it wasn't Wolf I was murdering.

"Okay," he called. Then I heard him chuckle. "What did you do?"

"Fucked up," Link said.

"Man, he's lookin' to kill you."

"At least I'd die by my man's hands," Link yelled.

The damn idiot.

I wasn't his man.

"I am not your man," I shouted.

Ruin's chuckle sounded, but it faded when I turned another corner.

"Ryo, baby, I'm sorry," Link called.

I shoved my door open and moved into my room, slamming it after me. I went to my wall and grabbed one of my blades, turning to face the door when it was pushed open.

Link blinked at me. "Baby?"

"You should pay for what you did."

He nodded straight way. "I know."

He didn't get it.

"You need to *pay* for what you did."

He cocked his head to the side. "What did I do?"

Jaw clenching, my heart hammered against my ribs as my ears rang.

No.

He didn't deserve my words.

Link stepped further in and shut the door after him before he faced me again. "Baby, what did I do?"

Lifting my hand, I pointed the tip of my blade his way. "You *will* pay for what you did."

He spread his arms wide and moved closer. "Okay, I'll pay. Cut me, mark me, make me bleed, but tell me what I'm paying for."

I ground my teeth together.

With a flick of my wrist, red coated his neck and cheek from the slight cuts I'd opened.

He didn't even flinch. "I'll take it. I'll take anything you give me, baby, as long as you talk to me."

I threw the sword to the ground, hands fisting at my sides. "You're a prick."

"I am."

"And annoying."

"Totally."

"I hate you," I clipped.

"I deserve it all, baby, but tell me what I need to pay for."

"No."

"Snook, come on. Tell me, please."

"No."

He pouted.

This grown man pouted as he pressed his hands together under his chin while begging, "Pretty please." I looked away and then felt his fingers under my chin, turning my head back. "Please, baby."

"Don't call me that."

"Why do I need to pay?" he asked softly.

I shoved at his chest, but he stayed where he was, brushing the backs of his fingers over my cheek. Blood seeped from the cuts I gave him. I watched it run down over his jaw.

"Baby—"

I pushed his hand away and glared. "Because you made *me* feel."

"Feel what?" He pushed against me, cupping my cheeks.

"Leave."

"Baby, what did I make you feel?"

"Fear," I admitted tightly.

"I'm sorry." He kissed my cheek. "I'm here." He kissed the other. "I'm okay." He pressed his lips to mine. "I won't do it again."

Reaching out, I gripped the back of his head and slammed my mouth onto his for a rough, hard, demanding kiss.

How fucking dare he make me fear losing him.

CHAPTER EIGHT

LINK

*T*he concern I'd held over fucking up royally vanished as soon as he took my mouth in a punishing kiss that had my cock thickening so damn fast.

He'd been scared, but what got to him most was that he'd hated the thought of losing me.

He liked me.

He fucking liked me a damn lot.

I wanted to crow at the sky in elation.

But I was too busy enjoying this moment.

He pulled his mouth from mine and grumbled something along the lines of, "Foolish idiot doesn't deserve this." Before he yanked my shirt up and over my body. He studied my arm where I got the scrape from a passing bullet before using my shirt to wipe over the cuts he'd made and dropping it to the floor to glare at me again.

However, it didn't last because he got distracted by my good looks.

His gaze slowly ran over my physique.

Oh, he liked what he saw.

Just like I loved every fucking inch of him and his hard shell.

"What do you want, snook?"

"Don't call me that."

I smirked. "Okay, baby."

His gaze narrowed once more. "Or that."

"What do you want?" I tried again.

"Control."

I spread my arms wide. "You have it. Do with me what you want."

His jaw clenched.

"You'd give your control up that easily?"

"Baby, for you, yes. No one else would have it or has had it."

"What happens if I want to fuck you?" He cocked his head to the side, which was fucking adorable, as was how he was still glowering at me for making him feel things he didn't want to admit to.

"Pound my ass all you want, baby."

He straightened, gaze flaring in shock.

He didn't get it.

But he would.

Taking his hand in mine, I led it up to my throat and pressed it against me. He tightened his grip.

"You and only you, Ryo, can do whatever you want to me. You've gotten under my skin in a way I don't want to remove. Fuck, I'd cut myself open and have you live inside me if I could. But for now, I'd settle with seeing and talking to you every damn day. Which I'm hoping will lead to bedroom activities real soon. But, again, I'm willing to wait, and when the time comes, I'd let you spank me, whip me, bite me, come all over me, fuck me in the mouth or arse because I wanna do all the dirty and sweet things with the man I'm obsessed with." As I leaned in, his hand gripped me but relaxed when I sucked on his ear lobe. "And you can do all that before you put a ring on my finger."

I expected a laugh, but it never came.

Instead, he used his hand on my throat to push me back, and when I had his hard gaze, he said, "What happens if I want you to do all those things to me?"

My blood boiled and cock ached.

Groaning, I cupped the back of his head and nipped at his bottom lip. "Then, snook, I'll do everything you want." I kissed the corner of his mouth. "You just gotta let me know what you want or tell me to lead, and until you do tell me, I'll be a good, patient boy, just for you."

He snorted, shaking his head. He dipped his chin low and looked up at me. "You've never been a good boy."

Grinning, I ran my hands up and down his sides. "Then I'll be your bad boy. Just yours."

"You're crazy."

"Crazy for you," I told him, because in all honesty, I really was insanely needy to have this man at my side all the damn time.

I didn't lie when I said he was the first person I thought of when we'd been shot at.

As if my thoughts reminded him, he glanced to the scrape, and his jaw clenched. "Who was shooting at you?"

"Doesn't matter. They're all dead."

"Who was it?"

"Some thugs who wanted to own some of my territory to run their girls." When his jaw clenched, I kissed him there. "Don't stress, snook. I'll make sure their girls are taken care of. They can come work for me, or my crew will help them find a job they want."

He nodded.

"Can I have another kiss?" I asked, pressing my lips to his neck.

"You seem to be doing fine without asking," he pointed out.

Chuckling, I licked up his neck and scraped my teeth over his ear lobe, which drew out a beautiful little shudder.

"Since you didn't say no, it's given me the green light to kiss you whenever I want."

"I—"

"Nah-ah, snookum," I said against his lips before I kissed him deep.

When we wrapped each other up in our arms, we held on tightly. Possessively. I grinned into the kiss until he sucked on my tongue, shooting a buzz of lust straight to my cock.

Christ, I wanted to climb down his throat and drown in all his blood.

Ryo suddenly shoved me back.

Panting, we stared at each other.

"Get undressed and on the bed," he ordered.

Holy shit.

Grinning, I quickly undid my slacks and shoved them and my boxers down my legs. I kicked my shoes off with my pants and removed my socks before I ran at the bed and jumped on.

In the middle of the mattress, I rolled to my back and looked at my still-dressed fantasy-come-true.

"Snook, you want a show or are you gonna join?" I slid a hand down my chest and stomach before I wrapped it around my erection.

He swallowed and removed his jacket. His shirt was next, and I couldn't wait to lick all over his beautiful skin.

Please, baby, let me leave my mark.

I wanted to suck my spot right over his heart.

Claim it as mine.

A moan dropped from my mouth when he shoved his pants and underwear down to reveal his hard cock.

"Am I gonna get to suck it, snook?"

"No."

I sat up, pouting. "But I wanna."

He sighed and pinched the bridge of his nose. Dropping his hand, he glared. "Lay back."

I dropped with my arms and legs out like a starfish as I watched my delicious and naked Ryo walk around the bed to his bedside table. He opened the first drawer and pulled out a bottle of lube.

"You gonna warm me up, love?" I didn't mind pain, but I liked butt play a heap. Giving and receiving. Fingers, tongue, lips.

He uncapped the lube and squirted some on his fingers before placing the bottle on the blanket. "No." He reached around to his ass. "I'll get myself ready."

Like fuck.

I shot up to my knees and begged, "Let me. Please, baby. I'll make you feel so good. Let me touch you. Let me stretch you, please."

His jaw clenched, but his cheeks pinked. He straightened and grabbed a couple of tissues from the stand before wiping his fingers clean.

"Fine."

"Fucking yes," I cried. I crawled on my knees over to him and kissed him deep and long. Rough and teasing. He took it all.

After a last nip to his bottom lip, I got to my feet and walked around him. I mouthed at his shoulder before I gently pushed him forward.

I licked and sucked at his waist and lower back, drawing out small sounds from Ryo.

My man felt tense, but when I brushed my fingers over his cock, I found it hard and hot.

Ryo pressed his fists to the bed and spread his legs.

I palmed each cheek and dropped to my knees behind him.

Sticking my tongue out, I swiped it over his pretty pink hole.

"Link," he bit out with a moan that he didn't allow all the way out.

"I've got you, baby," I told him right before I kissed my need and want against his hole, making it wet and relaxed. By the time I had two fingers in, fucking him, my beautiful, angry angel had mellowed enough to press his forehead to the bed and give me his horny noises that I wanted to drink down, but I was too busy eating.

"Enough," he said as he moved out of reach while his body trembled. "I need…."

Standing, I jerked my hand up and down my cock. "Tell me, baby."

"For you to not call me that."

"And?" I asked in hope he wanted me to bury my cock deep inside him.

A knock sounded on the door.

"Go the fuck away," I yelled.

"Ryo?" Wolf called.

"I'm gonna shoot your boss if he doesn't disappear," I told Ryo, and his pretty lips twitched.

"We'll be out shortly," Ryo called back.

"Not too shortly," I added.

We waited a beat and thanked fuck when no other knocks came.

"Link."

"Ryo," I countered.

"Will you have sex with me?" he asked all sweet and nice like.

"Baby, I'm gonna fuck you so good, you'll still feel me tomorrow."

He cocked a brow. "We will see."

I grinned. "Challenge accepted." I waved a hand to the bed. "Back or knees, baby, your choice."

He bit his bottom lip as he thought.

Damn cute.

He climbed onto the bed and rolled onto his back. Before he could second-guess this whole thing, I slid onto the mattress between his spread legs.

His face heated. "I should roll over."

Dipping, I pecked at his lips, nose, and cheeks. "Nah, baby. You're right where you should be."

This way I could watch him.

This way I could kiss him and make sure he knew who's the one fucking him.

"There's condoms in the night drawer." Another cute blush raced across his cheeks.

Resting back on my knees, I leaned over and pulled

a rubber free. After I rolled it on, I picked up the lube and applied more to his hole and my cock before throwing it down.

Stroking over my cock, I ran my gaze over him and grinned when I got to his glare.

"Hurry up," he snapped.

"One day we're taking our time. We're gonna build up to it all day long and fuck nice and slow where I'm rocking in and outta you until your ass milks my cock and drains me dry."

His lips parted, and he breathed heavy, imagining it.

"But right now, my baby wants to fuck, and he's gonna get my cock."

Placing one hand to the bed, I used the other to line my dick up with his hole and pushed in slowly.

His mouth opened, back arched, and he closed his eyes.

"Open those eyes, baby. Need you to see who's sliding into your tight little hole."

He opened them and glared.

Chuckling, I leaned down and took his mouth in a hot kiss of tongue and teeth and lips as my cock breached the tight muscle and I pushed deep, groaning at him fitting me snugly.

"Christ, baby, you feel so good." I drew back and pushed in. His moan swept down my throat as we kissed again.

"Link," he breathed.

I thrust in and out of him, slapping back and forth.

"Yeah, baby. I'm the one fuckin' you. Look at you taking me so damn well." He moaned, and I hissed out a breath as my balls drew up. "Fuck, snook, you feel… like you're mine."

His moan sounded with a growl of annoyance. "Faster, harder," he demanded.

I gave him what he wanted.

Snapping my hips back and forth. Fucking his sweet hole like my life depended on it while we kissed and licked.

Trailing my mouth down, I sucked at his skin. His fingers dug into my flesh, and knowing I'd have bruises tomorrow had me smiling. I pulled back, and goddamn pride settled into me at the sight of my mark on him.

He glanced down at his chest and groaned. "Link."

"Baby, wanna mark you all over," I told him as I fucked his sweet hole. "Wanna sweat and come on your skin and rub it in so everyone can smell me on you. Damn obsessed with you, baby."

"You… you prick," he moaned as he came, untouched, over his stomach.

"Fuck yes," I groaned, drilling in and out of his tightness and filling the condom as his hole milked everything out of me.

I gave him some lazy kisses, which he took and shared with me some soft touches.

When I pulled out of him, I rolled to his side and went up on an elbow. He closed his legs and rolled to face me but tucked his face under my chin in a shy manner.

Chuckling, I curled him into me more and hugged him tightly.

"I'm gonna stay the night," I informed him.

"No," he muttered grumpily.

"Too bad, snook. We're gonna hug for a bit, maybe watch a movie, eat dinner, and go to sleep together."

He sighed. "Why do you want to stick around?"

I kissed the top of his head. "Because I'm a needy fucker who wants his man's attention after coming hard." I nipped at his shoulder, and he tried to shove me away. "We should have a bath too."

"Link."

"I ain't saying it's for you. I want to relax back while holding you."

"No."

"Fine, we'll have a shower together. I might even suck your cock too."

He stilled. "Okay," he whispered eventually.

Fuck yeah, I was winning my man over.

CHAPTER NINE

RYO

"I will punch you in the throat if you keep staring at me," I threatened the man sitting on the couch next to me.

He hummed low and kissed my neck before chuckling in a way that made my pulse race. It reminded me of the noises he made while he was inside me.

He should have left.

He should be bored now that he had me.

If anything, sleeping with this man had made him worse.

He'd been glued to my side all afternoon.

Wolf had even told me to get out of his office when Link kept talking and touching things, since he didn't want to be far from me for some insane reason.

Link had also sent his bodyguard home, since he'd invited himself to stay the night and told Bradshaw to come back tomorrow morning.

"But I like staring at you," he simply said.

Sighing, I rolled my eyes, making sure that on the outside I looked put out from his attention, while on the inside, I was starting to like it.

And that sent my chest into a panicked flutter.

He made my body hum from everything he said and did.

Like now, how he absently traced his inked fingers up and down my arm.

Did he know how the action made my stomach flutter like it was on a roller coaster?

There was a knock before the door opened. I straightened and pulled my arm away as Katon stepped in.

He bowed. "Dinner will be ready in an hour."

I nodded once, and he disappeared back out the door.

If I faced Link, would I see him upset at me for pulling away?

I wasn't sure I could get used to being comfortable with him around other people. Maybe I would around Wolf and Ruin, but being affectionate in front of anyone else didn't sit right with me.

I was always the stoic one. The cold, stern assistant and personal guard to Taro-Sama "Wolf" Takahashi.

A warm hand settled on the middle of my back. "I'm already looking forward to all the food."

Looking over my shoulder, it was to see him smiling with a gentle gleam to his gaze.

My heart skipped a beat.

"Yes. There may be others from Wolf's family present too." Meaning there would be an audience, and I'd be on high alert.

He winked. "Promise I'll be on my best behaviour."

My lips twitched as humour rolled through me. "I have yet to see this best behaviour."

Chuckling, he reached up and swiped a finger along my jaw. "For you, baby."

"Don't call me that," I ordered, but with no real push.

He grinned.

This man.

He acted like he didn't have a care in the world, and maybe in his mind, he didn't, but all I saw was the danger, the risk, the judgements, the hate.

I wished I could be more like him, but I couldn't.

The way I was had saved Wolf on many occasions because I didn't trust easily.

Except, it seemed, with this man.

He leaned forward and pressed his lips against mine.

However, before the kiss could deepen, Link's phone rang. He pulled away, grinned, and yanked me back against him at the same time as he took his cell from his pocket and chuckled at the screen. "Missing me?"

For a moment, I tensed and wondered if it was one of his lovers.

But since I had Link stuck to my back, he felt me still.

"One sec, Trav." He muted the call and turned to me. "Baby?"

"Don't."

"Snook, it's just Travis. I always talk to him like that, but we've only ever been friends. The guy's as straight as they come."

I nodded, suddenly feeling foolish for my instant reaction.

Maybe I trusted him, but not others.

People would want his time and attention.

He kissed my neck before he unmuted the call. "Yo ho, what's up?"

"I heard the takeover of Wolf's clients isn't going as smooth as you hoped."

What?

Standing, I spun on him with my hands on my hips.

"Ah, shit, bro…. No, wait, I'm gonna get into trouble."

"Who is giving you trouble, Link?" I demanded. "How many? You will tell me. Did you lie about the thugs? Was it one of Wolf's clients who shot at you? I want names. Let me deal with them. Wolf still owns 10 percent, which means I can help." My hands tingled for a weapon.

I heard laughter come through the phone before Link said, "No. It's my boyfriend—"

"I am not your boyfriend," I snapped.

"Ryo. Yeah, Wolf's guy, but he's my guy now."

"I am not."

Link grinned. "No, no, I'm wearing him down. He'll love me in the end, and that's when I'll slide a ring on his finger."

I glared. "You will not." I waved a hand about. "Hang up. I want to know everything."

"Yeah, mate, we'll do dinner soon, and I'll bring him. Give Vi and Izzy a kiss for me."

When the call ended, he sat forward and threw his phone onto the coffee table behind my legs before he grabbed me and pulled me down to lay on the couch.

He got up and straddled my hips.

"Fuckin' love you being protective, but, baby, I've got a handle on it."

I glowered up at him. "You were shot at."

"I know." He leaned down and kissed my jaw. "Nothing I can't deal with, snook."

"Let me speak with Wolf's previous clients. They'll listen to me. They feared me."

He trailed his tongue up and down my neck.

It was hard to think.

My cock throbbed.

"And I'll make them scared of me too. Wolf may still own 10 percent, but he's a silent partner for a reason. He wants to keep his family safe. You're a part of that family."

"What about you?" I blurted.

It was lucky he pulled back to grin down at me, because I pulled my arm up to hang over my burning face.

"It doesn't matter," I tried.

"Oh no, it really does. Baby, are you asking for me to give up that world because you're scared for my safety?"

I threw my arm off and glared. "No. Do not be stupid." I shoved at him. He talked like he would already consider doing it for me, and that made me wild. Happy and angry, jittery and relaxed. Mixed up and messed up. I shoved at him again, but he grabbed my arms and held them to the couch above my head.

"It's all right, snook. We can table that. I get it. It's too serious and too soon for you."

"You don't know what you're talking about. Fuck me and get bored already," I demanded.

His grin turned devilish. "Never."

My heart bounded and leaped, knocking into my ribs. My ears rang with how fast my blood pumped through my veins.

He couldn't mean never.

He would grow bored and leave eventually.

And when that time came, I wasn't sure I would

survive the fall because this man made me feel too many things in such a short amount of time.

He'd crawled his way under my skin and dug his nails in to stay deep.

"Get off me," I whispered, emotions suddenly clogging my senses. I ground my teeth together and narrowed my gaze, blocking it all out.

"Baby." The way he softly and gently said it made me think he knew what I was thinking.

That he could destroy me.

"Off," I ordered.

He leaned in and kissed my cheek and then the corner of my mouth where he said, "I'm gonna climb off you, snook, but I want you to know I ain't going anywhere. I like you a hell'va lot, Ryo baby, *just as you are.*"

My body melted into the couch, and I closed my eyes.

Link hummed and kissed my jaw near my ear. "Yeah, I'll show you, lover, that I'm gonna stick to you in a way you'll never doubt I want to be at your side."

His weight lifted off me. Hopefully, he was unaware of how much he made me light up on the inside.

In a way I never had before.

I was *seen* with this man, and that choked me up.

"Come on, baby." I glanced to see him holding his hand out.

With a thick throat, I placed mine in his, and he helped me off the couch.

As I pulled my hand from his, I went to walk off, but an arm slid around my waist, and I felt his lips on the back of my neck.

"Last thing I'm gonna say before we hit dinner. Need you to remember you're the only one I'm involved with. I'd never answer a call like that to anyone other than a friend because I only want you in my bed and warming my heart like the way you are."

"Stop," I pleaded.

Suddenly I felt unable to hear any more nice and sweet words from him.

"You got it, baby." He pressed his lips to my shoulder before he stepped around me and took my hand, leading me to the door. "We should get to the dining room early, anyway. I ain't missing out on any of that good food." He rubbed at his stomach and then opened the door.

I removed my hand from his, but I couldn't look at him afterward.

I didn't want to see the disappointment.

Maybe I needed to tell him I couldn't be anything he wanted.

Stepping out of the room, I stopped. "Link, I…." How was I supposed to say it? "You…. I can't…." I would never be enough for him.

He deserved better.

Someone who could share and show their attraction and attention to someone they cared for in public.

Someone who wasn't me.

Link tapped his foot against mine twice, and when I brought my gaze up to his, he grinned. "Baby, you be you, and I'll come along for the ride, no matter. Don't stress, yeah? I'll take it all as it comes. In public, you lead. I'll be the best boyfriend—"

"You're not my boyfriend," I said, but I didn't have the heat behind my words this time.

I was tired of lying to myself, no matter how much it scared me.

Link grinned and tipped his chin at me. "Behind closed doors, I am."

My jaw clenched. "How could you settle for that? You deserve—"

"Hey, I ain't settling. You're worth everything."

I closed my eyes and turned my face away. "You don't know what you're talking about."

"All good, baby. One day you'll see."

I sighed. "See what?"

"See that we're gonna have the best life together."

Dear God, this man.

Shaking my head, I turned and started for the dining room. Link stepped up beside me and followed with a spring in his step.

He didn't care I walked in silence, and I liked that he didn't bother making small talk.

It was like he just enjoyed being close.

You idiot, he's proved that since he got here.

But *why* did he like being around me?

Seriously, why me? I didn't understand it. No one else wanted to stay or to understand me or to spend more time with me other than getting off.

Would I ever understand him?

CHAPTER TEN

LINK

Smitten. I was so fucking smitten, I wanted to punch myself in the face for being so cringe. My poor baby was a muddled mess inside his brain, and I was sure he was thinking I was unhinged for liking him. But I wasn't. I was only loco when it came to protecting my people and businesses; I'd kill any man or woman who fucked me over.

But I knew without a doubt that I was going to wear Ryo down and we'd live a happily-ever-after life.

After I killed all his family for making him think he wasn't worthy of someone's time and attention.

At the door to the dining room, I pushed it open for him and waved him through with a grin.

He glared and clenched his jaw, but I knew on the inside he was swooning for me.

The room was packed. I fucking hated how many eyes there were because I knew Ryo couldn't be himself. His shoulders pushed back as he stalked toward the head of the table where Wolf and Ruin were.

"Hey, I guess we didn't get here early enough. Lucky the food hasn't arrived yet," I commented as I followed Ryo, who hummed in return.

His reserved ways in front of people were cute.

Though, I bet it had to do with his family and how they brought him up, and it made me want to hunt them down and smother them with bags over their heads.

If they ever showed their faces around Ryo, I'd shoot first and ask questions later.

Still, the only good thing they did was bring Ryo into the world, because I wouldn't have met him otherwise.

Cheers to illegal activities.

"Hey," I called to Ryo's friends as I pulled out his chair while he bowed at Wolf. But then I saw the flare to Ryo's gaze, which was on the chair, so I quickly dropped down into the seat next to his.

"Link, I see Ryo got to you." Ruin tapped his cheek and neck.

I grinned. "I deserved it."

Ruin snorted before asking, "Heard you got shot at too."

I glanced at Ryo to see his jaw clench. "Ha, yeah. Just a little misunderstanding, but that was all sorted."

"I would like no talking about business at dinner," Wolf commented. "Katon," he called.

The older guy popped his head out of the swinging door at the back. "Taro-Sama?"

"Please let the kitchens know we're all ready."

"Of course." And he disappeared again.

As Wolf was drawn into a conversation with an older woman and Ruin spoke with Ryo, I took the chance to look along the full table. Family of Wolf's from all ages sat talking or looking at something on their phones.

No one questioned what I was doing here. No one gave me a strange look, like I shouldn't be here. They'd all just accepted my appearance.

It showed me that Wolf ran his family well. They knew to trust him.

"It wasn't always this peaceful at the dinner table," Ryo said softly beside me. When I turned to him, he went on. "Wolf had members who disrespected him and his life choices." His gaze flicked to Ruin. "They also made it clear they hated Wolf's sister."

I grunted. "She's a Hawks club girl, yeah?" I was sure I heard that somewhere.

"Used to be. She's dating a brother of the club."

"So what happened to those family members?"

"Punished by the law," Ryo said.

Wolf was setting his family up on the straight and narrow. Probably why he let the cops handle those members. Where if it'd been me, I would have wanted their blood coating my hands for betraying me.

Maybe Wolf did run his family well, but not everyone liked how he did it.

Were there problems within these walls still?

Was Ryo in trouble here?

"Anyone else in the family that needs to be watched?" I asked, gaze moving over the people slowly.

Fingers brushed over the top of my hand, and I looked back to Ryo, whose gaze held humour.

"What?"

He opened his mouth and closed it, shaking his head.

The doors at the back opened, and the staff rushed in with trays of food.

"Oh yeah, bring it on." I rubbed at my gut, almost drooling from the scent wafting around.

If Wolf wasn't a silent partner and I could spend more time here, I'd do it for the food alone.

Well, that and my snookums too.

As I piled my plate high, I asked, "Wolf, do you know if your neighbours would sell?"

"Why?" Wolf asked after he swallowed his mouthful.

Shit, it probably wasn't the best time to talk about buying it so I could be close to Ryo and have a secret passage to see him whenever I wanted. Plus, it'd be good to cut down the eyes on Ryo in case they noticed how much he meant to me. If we could hide it behind closed doors, then maybe my drama from the businesses wouldn't touch him.

Unless I also went on the straight and narrow.

Well, fuck me, that thought had never really crossed my mind. I may have said something to Ryo before, but it was a passing comment. Could I seriously give it all up for the man next to me?

Maybe.

If he wanted me too.

"No reason," I said quickly.

Ruin snorted and coughed out "Bullshit."

I scratched at my chin with my middle finger.

Wolf asked, "How old are you, again?"

"Age is just a number, baby."

Goddamn it.

I shouldn't have called him that.

I turned to Ryo, who gripped his knife a little too tightly.

"Ryo—"

"Wolf, you have two appointments tomorrow outside of the property. I'll make sure there's extra guards with me."

"Okay?" Wolf drew out slowly.

Fuck, shit. I knew calling Wolf baby was gonna rile my man. I hadn't meant it. It'd been a slip of the tongue.

As I went to eat, I rested my hand to Ryo's thigh and

squeezed. After I swallowed, I whispered out the corner of my mouth, "Won't happen again."

His gaze flicked to mine and then back to his plate, and I only relaxed when he nodded once. The rest of the table went on about random things while I sat and watched, only chatting when someone, mainly Ruin and Wolf, spoke to me.

I needed to watch what I said and did because I never wanted Ryo to second-guess about taking this chance on me.

He was prickly, but he was mine, and if I didn't take his emotions into consideration, then I'd be a fuckwit.

He was important, and I'd make sure he knew it, even when the truth scared him.

A smile tugged at my lips when I thought that if Ryo had a shell like a turtle, he would hide himself inside it any time I talked about feelings.

Which was fine with me.

I liked him as he was.

Sitting back, I watched as he chatted with Wolf. He'd dressed back in a suit after we'd had sex, while I'd borrowed jeans and a tee from him.

I wanted to see him naked again.

I wanted to mess up his perfectly styled dark hair after we'd been making out for a while.

Hell, I couldn't wait to sleep beside him in his bed.

Would he be the big spoon or the little? I reckoned I could talk him into becoming the little spoon, since I really liked the thought of covering him as much as I could with myself while we drifted off to sleep.

Ryo leaned back. "Stop staring," he bit out lowly.

I grinned. "Can't."

He rolled his eyes and picked up a napkin to wipe his mouth. "If you'll excuse me, I have things I need to see to."

When he stood, I pushed my own chair back. "What he said." I thumbed at Ryo to Ruin and Wolf before I moved to push my chair in. "Thanks for dinner."

Ruin tipped his chin up as he smiled, while Wolf nodded once, and then I rushed to catch up with Ryo, who was nearing the main entrance.

When I fell into step beside him, I asked, "Where're we going?"

"*I'm* going to speak with the team."

"Okay, I'll come."

"I wish you wouldn't," he muttered.

I grinned when he looked at me. "Noted and denied."

Unless he really wanted me gone, then I'd go and wait in his bedroom for him. I knew where that was.

Although, when he just sighed and said no more, I took that as a sign for me to follow along like a little loyal puppy—who'd hump his master's leg anytime he could.

Hell, my cock jerked under the jeans at the image of sucking Ryo's cock while I ground my aching dick against his leg.

He loved having my mouth in the shower; the sounds he made were locked away in the part of my brain dedicated to Ryo.

"What are you smiling about?"

"Humping your leg."

He stumbled, and I quickly reached out to stop him from falling. Of course, he shot me with a glare before walking on.

"Make sure I never ask you that again."

Chuckling, I brushed the back of my fingers against his. "That'll be a no. I like you knowing everything on my mind."

"Please, *don't* feel free to share your thoughts." His lips twitched.

Grinning, I told him, "But, baby—"

His face shut down of any emotion.

Grabbing his wrist, I pulled him to a stop.

He withdrew his arm to cross both of his over his chest. "I have things I need to do."

"In a sec."

People rushed by. I didn't have a clue who they were, but I waited for them to be out of earshot while Ryo clenched his jaw.

"Look, I'm gonna fuck up like that shit with Wolf, calling him what I do you, but you gotta understand that it means something totally different when I say it to you."

He stared off down the hallway. "It shouldn't matter."

Blow up my heart, he was annoyed he was jealous, while I fucking loved it.

"It does matter. If I do it again, fucking kick me or something. I hate irritating you or making you feel like you aren't my special snook when—"

"Oh my God, please shut up." Blushing, he covered his eyes with a hand.

Chuckling, I tapped at his chin, and when I had his eyes, I said, "If we weren't at risk of being spotted, I'd totally kiss you right now."

He let out a snort that sounded half scoff and half annoyed groan.

It was cute.

"I think you need to see a doctor."

"Of love."

He blinked before screwing up his nose. "Ew."

Spluttering out a laugh, I asked, "Did you just *ew* me?"

His lips twitched. "You were too corny."

Grinning, I nodded. "All right, I'll give you that. Now let's get this done so we can go to bed and snuggle."

"I do not snuggle." He glared, turned, and stalked off. But it wasn't as fast as before and almost like he wanted to wait for me to catch him.

Fuck yeah, I was growing on him.

CHAPTER ELEVEN

RYO

I wanted to wrap my hands around this man's throat and choke him for being… adorable. I'd never slept beside anyone until now, and the noises he made were too sweet for his own good. He was melting me in ways I'd never experienced, and I wanted to kill him for making my heart react.

But I also wanted to smother him with a pillow so he'd stop fluttering my stomach from those little puffs he made with his mouth.

Since I really didn't want him dead—at least I think I didn't—I went back to watching him.

He was in my bed.

Even when I'd offered the spare room next to mine,

he'd ignored it and walked into my room to strip and slip under my covers.

Like he had every right to do so.

I thinned my lips so I didn't laugh when he snuffled a little.

Wait….

Why was he making that noise?

Was there something wrong with his mouth? His lungs? His face? Did he have a sleeping disorder? I hadn't noticed if he stopped breathing or not, but I hadn't been awake long either.

Did he need to see a doctor?

Sitting, I reached for my phone. Maybe Wolf would know.

An arm curled around me, and I was dragged back down under a warm body as it covered me.

"Where were you going?" Up on his elbow, he hovered over me with a small smile and tired eyes.

My gaze travelled all over his tattooed neck, shoulders, and arms. His ink was always something I admired. He looked scarily hot.

What was he doing to me?

He brushed his nose against mine and then pushed his fingers through his messy salt-and-pepper hair to push it back.

"Your breathing was obnoxious and worrisome. I thought you might need a doctor."

His neck stretched as he roared in laughter. He

dipped his face down and pressed his forehead to my shoulder while he still chuckled.

"No, I am serious. You might need to see a doctor. You could have a sleep disorder that could kill you."

I felt his grin against the skin of my neck before he kissed there.

"Love that you're worried, snook, but I've lived through sleeping all these years already. I should be fine."

I sniffed. "If you think so."

When he scraped his teeth over the flesh of my neck, I bit my bottom lip to stop the moan wanting to spill free.

"Yeah, I'm sure, baby, and now I've got you to keep an eye on me."

"We won't be in bed together all the time."

He pulled back and grinned down at me.

Oh.

I realised my mistake too late.

"Not that we will be doing this again."

"Nah-ah, love. No take backs. We may not be in bed together all the time. But a *lot* of it. Which reminds me, I need to pay your neighbours a visit."

My chest expanded.

He couldn't mean....

"What for?"

"I wanna buy one of their places and start on that secret tunnel."

I shoved at his chest hard. "You're being ridiculous." When he flopped back, I sat up and leaned against the headboard to cross my arms over my chest. "This is just new. You're not going to want to stick around when you see I have the emotions of a dead fish, Link. I'm wired differently. I can't give you what you want, so please just forget this and stop acting like we'll last forever."

Link groaned, throwing an arm across his eyes, and my blood cooled.

Now he was finally understanding.

Any moment he would get out of bed and leave me. I'd never see him again.

An ache started in my chest, and I wanted to hurl, but I ignored it and waited.

It was for the best that he left.

It was.

He groaned again.

"I told you this was useless. Just go." I swallowed thickly.

He sighed.

But said nothing, and that agitated me even more.

He should be walking out by now.

When he blew out another breath and shook his head, I asked, "What are the noises for? I told you we wouldn't work."

He removed his arm and stared up at me. "I'm pissed."

My eyes bugged out. "It's not my fault you don't listen."

"I'm not pissed at that, baby. I'm fuckin' livid that I haven't done a good enough job at getting you to see we're in this for the long haul. If it wouldn't scare you, I'd shove my ring on your finger right now so every goddamn person knows who you belong to. Don't think I don't see some of the staff eyeing you like they wish they were in your bed."

He was crazy.

Absolutely insane.

How did he come up with this?

"I really do think you need to see a doctor or a psychiatrist."

He chuckled and sat up to lean against the headboard next to me. Of course, he practically glued himself to my side.

He kissed my shoulder.

I sighed. "Link—"

"Not having it, snook."

"What?"

He wound an arm across my stomach as he pressed into my side more and kissed my shoulder again. "I've told you before and I'll tell you again. No matter what you say or how you act, I like you the way you are. We're not just hooking up for the time being. We're dating in the way where we'll be in each other's future. I get that it's scary, but we'll work it out together."

My heart hammered into my ribs so fast, I was sure they would break.

This man.

He's crazy.

Utterly ridiculous.

But maybe that was just what I needed in my life because for some absurd reason he wanted us to work and he wasn't folding when I tried to push him away.

Could I risk getting hurt?

Or destroyed, since I believed that being with this man and having it end would wreck me.

As I turned my head to stare at him, he gave me a soft smile, causing my pulse to race.

He was insistent and serious, but playful and sweet.

I wanted to trust him with everything.

Even my heart.

I moved my gaze to the end of the bed when I said, "Okay."

Link scrambled to his knees and planted his hands on my shoulders and shook me.

When I looked up at him, he seemed like a child who saw his presents on Christmas morning for the first time.

"Okay? You said okay. That mean yes. No fuckin' take backs, snook. We're locked in. I'm gonna date the hell outta you."

And suddenly I was scared.

I cocked a brow. "Do you mind if we keep a lot of it behind closed doors?" My heart wouldn't be able to take Link's type of public displays of affection.

He leaned forward and claimed my mouth in a hard kiss.

"Anything," he said against my lips, and then I let out a gasp when he moved back and yanked me down along the mattress so he could straddle my waist.

"We gotta celebrate. You want my dick in you or you wanna fuck me?"

My cock jerked.

Both ideas sounded nice to me.

But I couldn't pick.

I wished I could slide inside his heat and have him fill me at the same time.

My face ignited with what I wanted to tell him, but I pushed the nerves down and spewed, "I haven't been with anyone since my last test, which was all good."

His smiled was slow and wicked. "Baby, are you telling me you wanna go ungloved?"

I wanted to fan my face but didn't. Instead, I nodded.

"Christ," he clipped, gaze darkening. "I'm good, too, snook, but now it's gotta be me fuckin' you so I can spray your insides with my cum." He hummed low. "Yeah, I fuckin' love the thought of that."

I did too.

A lot.

"Okay," I whispered.

He groaned, leaned down, and kissed me with tongue, teeth, and lips. Like he poured all his soft and sweet emotions, mixed with his dirty thoughts, into the kiss.

When he pulled back, both of our chests rose and fell rapidly.

"I gotta take a quick piss, though it might not be too quick, since I gotta wait for my cock to go down. You wanna come piss with me, or are you good?"

"Are we already at the stage in this relationship where we talk about bathroom visits?"

He grinned and then chuckled. "Baby, when you're with a guy like me, yeah we are."

I huffed. "Fine." My cheeks heated. This wasn't something I spoke about. "I'll go first so then I can shower and… prepare my body."

He smirked. "Snook, don't feel like you have to shower and clean your ass out. That don't bother me."

"Dear God, Link. We *don't* talk about *that*."

Another laugh left him. "Why not? It's your ass I fuck."

"Yes, but… cleaning isn't spoken of."

He snorted and rolled off me. "Baby, go do what you want to do, and I'll go take a piss in another bathroom, since there's billions around here. We'll meet back in bed in ten." He clapped his hands and yelled, "Let's go." He scrambled off the bed and bounced to his feet, but when he saw I hadn't moved, he cocked a brow.

"Are you always this energetic in the mornings?" I asked.

"Only when I've got a hot guy I'm gonna get a bit from."

Shaking my head, I shoved the blankets back and

climbed out of bed. "I think I need to evaluate my own head."

His abrupt, rough laugh had me jolting, and as he was on his way to the door, he said, "Already told you, baby, no take backs. We're stuck together now."

He opened the door and walked out, but it was then I realised he only wore a pair of my black boxers.

Grabbing a robe, I pulled it on as I rushed after him. When I stuck my head out the door, I bit out low and harsh, "Link."

He had his hand on the doorknob a couple down, and he turned back, smiling.

Always smiling or grinning or smirking.

This man.

"You need clothes," I snapped.

"Baby, I'll be back soon, and then even these will be gone."

Oh my God.

"Link," I warned.

His chuckle had me wanting to punch him. But then he looked over my shoulder and tipped his chin up. "Hey."

My blood froze over.

Woodenly, I turned to look down the other end of the hall.

Wolf and Ruin stood there with smug expressions that I wanted to wipe off their faces.

I bowed to Wolf and ordered, "Not a word."

"But—"

"No."

As I turned and started to close the door, Wolf called out, "I'll tell the cooks to leave some breakfast for you both *later*."

I clenched my teeth but managed to get out, "Thank you," then shut the door and stalked to the bathroom.

I had a man I needed to get ready for.

My man.

My *boyfriend*.

My stomach fluttered, and I felt like I was going to throw up, but I pushed through the nerves because I'd admit he was mine even when he drove me up the wall.

CHAPTER TWELVE

LINK

ONE MONTH LATER

"Jesus motherfuckin' Christ, baby." I slid my fingers into Ryo's hair as he sucked my dick like a damn Hoover. "You make me feel so good. Love your mouth, snook. Love your arse too. And your face. Hell, all of you is my top—teeth," I warned when he suddenly bit down on my erection.

He pulled off and warned, "I need you to fill my mouth so I can make this meeting."

Snorting, I told him, "I was working on it."

He stood with a glare and undid his pants. "You come faster when you fuck me. We're doing that."

"But I haven't prepped you. I ain't just gonna shove it in and hurt you."

His pretty face heated. "Don't worry about that." He pushed his pants and boxers down, kicking them away. With his knees to the couch, he pulled his shirt up to hold it in front of him and pressed his chest to the back of the cushions, jutting his arse out for me.

"Goddamn, snook, you look hot."

"Link," he whined.

I stood. "I'm gonna fuck you so good, baby." My gaze travelled down between his sweet globes to see something plastic and red sticking out of his hole. Groaning low, I palmed my cock. "You did this for me?"

"Yes. Now fuck me."

Yanking off my tee, I pushed my jeans all the way down and kneeled on the edge behind him, between his spread legs. We'd already been dressed for the day but had gotten carried away when we were kissing on the couch.

Threading my fingers through the top of his hair, I dragged his head back to my shoulder and used my free hand to grip the butt plug. "You needed your man able to fuck you whenever you wanted."

He moaned.

"Tell me," I ordered, sucking on his ear lobe.

"Yes. I always want you inside me."

A groaned growl dropped from my lips, loving he

shared that, as my cock throbbed. Slowly, I pulled the plug free and threw it onto the couch before forcing him, with a hand to his back, to lean over the couch more. "Gonna fill you up, baby. Fuck you hard."

"*Please.*"

I grabbed a packet of lube from the drawer next to the couch. Fucking glad I stocked up around my joint for this type of thing to happen. My man was wild in the bedroom or living room or dining. Hell, he wanted to be fucked all over the place.

My beau had my arse too. Only a handful of times because he preferred to bottom, which didn't bother me in the slightest. I fucking loved the thought of my cum swishing around his insides, marking him in ways no one else could.

And if anyone tried, I'd slaughter them.

Pressing in, I groaned from the way he moaned out my name. "Link."

"I got you, baby." Withdrawing from within his tight heat, I thrust my hips forward. Both of us made deep grunting noises.

Then, I did as my man had asked: I fucked him.

Leaning over him, I nipped and licked at his neck while I slammed my cock in and out of his hole.

My snookums loved hard and fast fucks.

But there were a few slow and romantic moments when I got to move at an easy pace in and out of him while we kissed and watched each other get off.

"Link," he whimpered.

"Yes, my good boy. Love fuckin' your tight hole. It's gonna milk me so right." I hummed against his shoulder and scraped my teeth over his flesh.

I wanted to gobble him up.

"Fuck, baby." A tingle rushed down my spine to my balls. "Gonna fill you, snook. You want my cum?"

He nodded, glanced over his shoulder with his sultry eyes. "I need it."

Fuck yeah, my dirty man.

"Baby," I groaned, spilling inside him.

His arse squeezed around me, milking out every drop, as he cried out, "Link," and came over the leather couch.

Hugging him from behind, I did a slow roll of my hips to push my cock in once more while I mouthed at his shoulder and neck.

He turned his head my way, and I knew what he wanted. I met his lips with my own and licked over them before sucking on his tongue.

"Christ, baby, I'll never get enough of you." Slowly, I pulled out, which caused him to shiver.

Standing, I bent to see some of my seed leak out of his reddened hole and drew my gaze up to his glaring eyes. "Can I stand now?"

"Can I get a picture now?"

He let out a quick laugh as his cheeks burned. "No." He stood, letting his shirt fall over him. "I'll clean the couch."

"Leave it, snook. I'll grab it. You go get ready."

He hesitated, glancing from his cum to me and back.

Then he stepped up to me and kissed my jaw before walking away.

I grinned like a maniac.

The joy I felt in those soft moments he gave me were fucking pure and melted my damn corrupt heart. He didn't initiate intimacy very often, but when he did, it was like he gave me something so fucking special each time.

Over the last month, and mainly in private, he'd given me more of himself, and I loved learning everything I could about him.

We were still careful when we stayed at each other's places. I'd been reckless when I'd showed up after getting shot at that day. Anyone could have followed. I hadn't fucking thought about it until the next day, and I'd been furious with myself.

Now, we took longer ways to get there to make sure no one was watching on. There were also two other cars, like our own, as distractions in case.

Ryo seemed to think I was going overboard, since he used to deal with the type of people in my world. But I wanted him safe. Plus, it was his boss who sold me a better portion of the shady dealings for a cleaner life.

Again, thinking these things had me wondering if I'd pull a Wolf or Travis and sell for the man I was loving.

I did love him.

I didn't want to go a day without seeing him, and when I had to, it was the fucking worst.

As I cleaned, I grinned at the thought of when Bradshaw called Ryo, demanding he come see me because he was sick and tired of hearing my whiny little voice when I complained of how many hours I hadn't been in Ryo's presence.

At least he'd come to visit that night after moving a few meetings around.

I didn't think Wolf would still be as busy as he'd been when he had the full run of the drugs and guns trade, but I'd learned quickly the man had many other businesses that kept Ryo working at Wolf's damn side all the time.

Which reminded me; I was waiting on a—my phone rang, I quickly went to grab it from the coffee table.

"Link," I answered.

"We'll take your offer," the man on the other end said.

"Fuckin' perfect. My team will be in touch. Thirty-day settlement."

"Yes," he said before he hung up.

Ryo was gonna be thrilled and pissed at the same time, and I couldn't wait to see his face screw up in frustration while his gaze warmed and he swooned.

Not that I'd tell him just yet. I had plans to woo him over dinner, get him all melty for me, and then I'd inform him I owned the house to the left of Wolf's.

I'd approached both neighbours a few weeks ago and asked what it'd take for them to sell their property. The one on the right wanted nothing. They were happy there. The one on the left took one look at me and my tatts through the camera at their front gate before telling me to fuck off and then ignored my insistent buzzing.

Bradshaw had to drag me away before I pulled my gun out and started shooting shit.

I'd made my accountant contact the guy to let him know I had enough money and assets to cover whatever he'd want and asked if he'd take my call.

Eventually, the old man was curious enough to listen to me. His wife wanted a new house to move into, and he wanted one of those fancy fucking yachts to go along with the obscene amount of money they wanted for their house.

I had a house that I needed to get rid of, and buying a yacht was easy enough. I'd agreed and sent him details of each item, then given him a time and date for when he had to give me his final answer.

Now we had a fucking deal.

Yippy fuckin' skippy.

I was damn pumped to get this show on the road.

When I met Ryo in the kitchen, he stopped and stared at me.

His gaze narrowed. "Why do you look so happy?"

"Baby, I'm always happy."

"Link—"

"Anyway, you better get going to make this meeting."

He glanced to the clock on the wall and then nodded. "You're right." He eyed me some more. "We'll speak later?"

"You got it. I'm coming to you this time." Only what he didn't know was that I'd be taking him to the same restaurant we'd met at for dinner so I could give him the good news.

Just in case he wasn't as thrilled as I was, I'd make sure there was nothing sharp close by.

Wolf knew I was going to take Ryo out, since I wanted to make sure I had his whole attention for the night.

"All right." He studied me some more. "I'm leaving."

"See you later, snook."

His hands slapped to his waist. "What's wrong?"

Snorting, I asked, "Nothing, what's wrong with you?"

"Usually, you would maul me a few more times before I even reached the front door, and yet today you're going to wait in the kitchen while I leave without.... Never mind," he snapped the last part and turned.

Chuckling, I called, "Baby, wait. You want more kisses, I can give them to you." Stalking after him, I cornered his body against the front door and manoeuvred him around to face me. "Sorry, I just had something on my mind. Give me some love, baby."

He turned his mouth away. "No. You're acting weird."

"I promise I'll explain everything tonight. I just don't want to make you late. I know how you hate it when you are."

He sighed. "Okay." He turned to me and kissed me, wrapping his arms around my waist and pulling me against him. I groaned into his mouth and twined my tongue around his, wanting to drink him down.

Fucking loved his mouth.

Loved everything about him.

After giving his jaw one last peck and nip, I said, "See you tonight."

"Yes," he replied softly.

Stepping back, I grinned and winked. He glowered and left.

I missed him as soon as he wasn't around.

And the guy thought I'd grow bored. There was no chance in hell. I was head-over-shoes taken by that man.

He'd see that tonight when I gave him the news.

After a shower, I made my way into the living room where I'd left my phone, arriving just as it rang.

I rushed around the couch to grab it, and when I saw Wolf's name, my gut tightened.

Had something happened?

"Wolf?"

"Ryo's family is in town and have demanded a meeting with him."

"You're not letting—"

"Ryo will not hide from them. He'll want to know what they want."

"Is this the meeting he had to be home for?" My gut clenched at the thought of him already knowing these fucks were showing and not telling me.

"No. That was something else that I've had to cancel."

"Does Ryo know they're showing, then?"

"Yes. I rang him just before you."

"When will they be there?"

"Ryo may not want you here. I was ringing so you'd be there for him after it."

"When, Wolf?" I clipped.

"In an hour."

"I'll be there. Let Katon know to direct me as soon as I arrive, and make sure the guards know I'm on my way."

"Link—"

"No one is stopping me from coming, Wolf. Ryo is mine. I take care of what's mine even against his own fucking family. If Ryo gets pissed over me showing, I'll deal with that later. But I'm gonna be there for him."

I pulled the phone away to make sure the call was still connected when Wolf didn't say anything.

"They are no longer his family. We are."

"Damn fucking right," I growled out and ended the call.

Finally, I was gonna get to face these motherfuckers.

They were gonna pay in one way or another for messing with Ryo and giving him trauma.

I went back to my bedroom and grabbed another gun.

I glanced down at my vintage Metallica tee and jeans. I'd dressed for a day in my home office, not out and about, but I wasn't changing now when I needed to make sure I arrived close to the start of this damn meeting.

Traffic had better not get in my goddamn way.

Walking to the intercom, I pressed it. "Bradshaw."

"Boss?"

"I'm heading to Ryo early. Set up the cars. I'll be in the garage in five. And Bradshaw, I want all the information you can on Ryo's family, the Satos from Japan. You'll fill me in on the road."

"Yes, sir."

My grin was one of savage delight.

CHAPTER THIRTEEN

RYO

My jaw ached from how hard I clenched. With every step I took, the louder my thoughts got, each one dragging up an unwanted memory of their cruel words and punishing blows.

The air felt heavy and thick, which added to my tension.

I didn't want to face them, and yet, I needed to find out why they wanted this meeting.

They gave no notice or time, just expected Wolf to drop everything for this to happen, and that aggravated me more than anything.

For my family, hesitation wasn't tolerated and obedience was expected before the command even finished being spoken.

That may be correct back in their hometown, but here, they didn't rule.

At the door to the office, I forced my features into a calm indifference and knocked once.

"Enter," Wolf called.

The tightness around my heart lessened when I saw my father and brothers weren't in the room with him.

I bowed. "Where are they?" I asked. I'd quickly gone to my room to change into my best suit and holstered two guns in case blood needed to spill.

"On their way up. Are you sure—"

There were a few sharp raps on the door.

I nodded. "Yes, Taro-Sama."

Wolf gave me a soft smile. I rarely called him that, and he knew that doing it now showed him my loyalty and how our trust went both ways.

"You are my friend and family, Ryo. I won't allow them to walk over you."

A bang sounded on the door. I glared over at it.

"I won't either."

Wolf nodded. He twisted to face the entrance, and I stood behind his chair with my hands clasped at my back.

"Enter," Wolf called.

I locked every emotion away and ignored the pounding to my heart when the door opened and my oldest brother, Kenta, stepped through first to check the room was safe before moving to the side for my father. The second oldest brother, Kazuya, brought up the rear.

"Take a seat," Wolf ordered.

They looked the same, but older, of course.

I thought I would feel intimidated or something from being near them, but there was nothing.

They'd become strangers to me, and I wanted to keep it that way.

Their gazes kept flicking my way as they sat in the chairs in front of Wolf's desk.

"What is it you want?" Wolf asked.

"Our brother can't even greet his father?" Kenta glared.

"Why should he?" Wolf asked.

When Kenta went to open his mouth, Father's grunt silenced him, and then he said, "We wish to speak with Ryo alone."

Wolf snorted. "That won't happen. Whatever you want to say will be said in front of me. Ryo is, after all, my employee."

"Your slave," Kazuya muttered.

Wolf's gaze snapped to him.

"*Loyal* employee, but more importantly, he is a friend and a part of my family."

The three of them glowered.

"Say what you have to say in front of Wolf and leave," I demanded.

Father's jaw clenched. He was furious.

The door suddenly opened, and Ruin stalked in. He went straight over to Wolf with a smirk on his lips.

I glanced at all three men opposite us to see they had their eyes glued to the tough-looking man wearing a motorcycle cut.

Wolf tipped his chin up as Ruin got close. My heart clenched.

Could I ever be this open with Link?

"Pet," Wolf whispered as Ruin bent and kissed him.

Ruin straightened, winked at Wolf, and moved over to lean against the wall.

"I had heard you disgraced your father's memory by bringing a man into your bed and house," my father said with a sneer.

"You do not speak to Wolf like that," I ordered, hands dropping to my sides, fists clenching.

Kenta scoffed. "Don't speak to your father that way."

"Have we found out what these guys want?" Ruin asked, sounding almost bored.

My father stuck his nose in the air. "I refuse to speak with *that* present."

I started to reach for my weapon, until Wolf lifted his hand. "Watch how you talk about Ruin around me, or I will make you leave. I didn't have to agree to this meeting. Say what you need and get out."

My family exchanged a look, expressions tight.

Father sighed. "It is time for my son to come home."

I tensed. He couldn't be serious.

They'd *sold* me.

"No," Wolf replied.

"The amount that was paid wasn't nearly enough for the years he's been here."

"He will not be leaving," Wolf stated.

Father ignored him and met my gaze. "For once in your life, do right by this family."

When had they done right by me?

I had a life here. One that was finally bright because of the man in it. There wasn't a chance I would leave Link.

Or Wolf.

Before I got to tell them this, the door banged open, making my family jolt, and my heart jump into my throat when I saw who stood at the threshold.

Link wore jeans and a tee, no shoes, and I had never seen that look of fury on his face before.

My cock throbbed, but now *really* wasn't the time.

Why was he here?

"These the fuckin' cunts?" he asked Wolf, who nodded.

My body warmed. He was here because my meddling friend told him about the meeting.

He was here for me.

The man looked menacing as he stomped further into the room to stop at the edge of Wolf's desk at the other end from where I stood.

Ruin watched him with a grin. Even Wolf's lips were twitching.

"These guys are Ryo's so-called family?" he asked again.

"Yes," Wolf answered.

As if slow motion existed, my eyes widened and my pulse spiked as I watched Link pull a gun free, aim, and fire three rapid shots at my family.

Shouts and cries echoed around the room as blood pooled from their upper arms.

Kenta went for his weapon.

"Stop," I snarled, drawing my own.

Ruin also had his out and pointed, but it was Link who darkly demanded, "Go on, move. I fuckin' dare you." He ground his teeth together, waiting and probably wishing they would move again so he could shoot them once more.

I shouldn't have found this highly arousing, but I did. My ears didn't just ring from the shots, but from how hard my blood sped through my veins, aiming for my cock.

Inappropriate, and yet, I didn't care.

This was the Link who ran his illegal trade.

He'd said he wanted to kill my family for what I'd shared with him, and now I honestly believed he wanted justice for me.

He was getting it too.

"Who are you?" Kenta asked, voice strained from the pain he would be feeling.

"Name's Link. Fuckin' remember it because I'll be the one making your lives miserable."

"You allow this?" Father demanded, flicking his gaze from me to Wolf.

Wolf waved a hand around. "I have no control over Link. Especially when he's pissed."

With a frantic heartbeat, I moved over to stand beside a furious Link and placed my hand on his back.

Link drew in a deep breath at my touch.

He had probably been worried that I'd be offended or annoyed over him showing here. But I wasn't. I couldn't be.

Wolf cared for me, but even he wouldn't go against my family. Back in Japan, they were the highest ruling family in the gun and drug trade. They'd been happy when Wolf's father moved his dealing to Australia and I went along with them.

But Link didn't care about anything but teaching my family a lesson for their treatment of me.

My family had looks of disgust on their faces.

"What is this?" Father clipped.

"This is your only fuckin' warning," Link told them, his voice harsh, low, and dangerous. My stomach fluttered, and I watched his side profile, witnessing the vicious look he showed them. "Ryo doesn't exist to you anymore. You think about contacting him in any goddamn way or form, I'll hunt you motherfuckers down and kill you all."

Kenta stood, wincing and holding his bleeding arm. "You can't order us."

Kazuya nodded and glared. "We have many at our back—"

"And I have fuckin' millions," Link bit out. "But no matter how many there are, I'll still be the one to get to you if you don't leave here now and never contact Ryo again."

"Why do you do this for him?" my father asked.

Link's lips thinned.

He wouldn't tell them we were lovers.

My gut churned.

He'd come here for me.

He stood up to them for me.

He meant more to me than anyone else had.

He showed me I deserved to be wanted and needed and cared for in ways that had me falling for this man.

For him, in this moment, I could be strong.

"He does it because he cares for me, like I do him," I told them, tipping my chin up slightly.

Link turned his body my way but still held his gun pointed at my family.

"Baby," he whispered.

Sighing, I faced him, lips twitching at the brightness to his eyes. All the fury he'd been feeling had vanished. "Don't overreact—"

"You care for me? I goddamn knew you'd fall for my awesomeness." There was a sound of someone shifting. "Move again, and I'll shoot you," Link warned, not looking away from me.

"I think this meeting is done," Wolf said.

Ruin grunted. "Tell Link you'll never contact Ryo again and leave."

Link grinned at me. "Can I shoot them again before they go? Or you wanna shoot them, snook?"

I smiled. "Not today."

"Fuck, baby, that smile…. We gotta hit your room."

Ruin and Wolf chuckled.

"You can't—"

"Kenta," Father clipped.

I turned to them. "I know the only reason you want me back is because it benefits the family in one way or another. Whatever it is, forget about it happening. I'll never leave here."

"Damn right," Link added, crowding my back and kissing my neck.

The disgust was clear to see on their faces once again.

"You're a disgrace—" Father cried out as his body jolted back in the chair when Link fired off another shot, hitting him lower on the arm.

"I can kill them all if you want," Link said into my ear before he kissed there. He wrapped an arm across my chest and held me tightly to him.

Reaching up, I smoothed my hand up and down his inked forearm. "No. I want them alive to know that I'll be living a happy and rich life with—"

"The one you care about," Link finished for me, and I felt his grin against my neck.

Smiling, I turned my head and kissed his jaw.

He beamed at me.

Like I'd just given him the best gift I ever could.

Or like a devoted puppy to his master.

Wolf picked up the phone. "Send a team in to escort the Sato family from the premises, and let it be known that if anyone sees them lingering in our area, they have permission to shoot and kill." Wolf replaced the receiver and crossed his arms over his chest.

"Means get the fuck out," Ruin supplied.

The door opened, and Link unglued himself from me as guards rushed in. I didn't even have time to panic about them seeing us in that type of position. Link acted before I could.

"Just remember what I said," Link warned my family as they were taken from the room.

Ruin walked over and shut the door before he turned back to us. "Do you think they'll listen?"

Wolf snorted. "I have a feeling they will."

Ruin grinned. "Cool moves, Link. Never thought you'd just show and shoot."

Link shrugged, winking at me. "When I'm pissed for someone I care about, I lose it a little."

"A little?" Wolf asked.

"Babe," Ruin said. "With the way they're lookin' at each other, I think we gotta leave the room."

"That is not happening, pet. This is my office. No one is doing anyone over my desk but you and me."

"I'm gonna take Ryo with me for the rest of the day," Link told them while staring at me.

"Yes, fine," Wolf said.

"But—" I started.

"No, no. Go with your needy man, or he'll be annoying for the rest of the day," Wolf told me. Ruin laughed.

My lips twitched.

He really would be annoying.

And now that he knew I cared for him, he'd become even more attentive, but he would also want my attention for him alone.

"Okay," I said.

Link smirked at me before he rushed toward the door, not knowing I was a bundle of nerves because I wanted to tell him exactly how much he meant to me.

CHAPTER FOURTEEN

Fuck yes, my snook finally admitted he had the hots for me. Now I just had to get him to see we were totally in love and that he'd be silly not to move in with me.

Shit. I needed to get contactors in to work on the tunnel as soon as the settlement was complete.

Dammit. I had to check with Wolf that he'd be down with that type of thing.

Then again, I had a good feeling he would be. He was all for marrying his friend off to me. I hadn't confirmed it, but I was nearly positive.

Ryo walked silently beside me to his bedroom.

I couldn't wait to get him behind closed doors.

Back in the office, when I first rocked up, worry had nearly eaten my organs from the thought of pissing him off by arriving and shooting those motherfuckers. But it worked out to be the right thing in the end.

Ryo revealed his feelings and showed me off to those so-called family cunts.

Man, I wanted to find and shoot them again.

They hadn't suffered enough.

I hated that they'd hid their pain. Hell, maybe I should've aimed for their—

Ryo suddenly pulled me to a stop with his hand around my wrist, which he quickly released, and when I faced him, he asked, "What are you thinking?"

"About shooting your family again."

His gaze softened. Hesitantly, since people were around, he reached out and brushed his fingers over the back of my hand.

"They received your message, and it was a pleasure to see you make them bleed for how they were to me. But they're not important."

No, you are.

I nodded. "All right, snook. I'll try not to picture putting more holes into their bodies when I think they deserve nothing but death."

His gentle smile had my heart skipping a beat. He started walking again, and I fell into step as he said, "Don't you see? They'll suffer more knowing I'm alive and happy and sleeping with the man who made them look like fools."

"Yeah, I guess. I had Bradshaw search for information on them so I'd know why they wanted to see you, but he couldn't find anything. Not in the time we had."

"They just wanted me back home to use me again for either connections or business." He tangled a finger with mine and tugged. "But that's not something we need to worry about now, and I would prefer not to talk about them again."

If he wanted to move on, then he got that.

"Sure, baby. They're forgotten."

We turned the hall to Ryo's room and made it the rest of the way in silence. But I kept catching him glancing my way.

What was on his mind?

His cheeks pink, he caught my slow grin, which made him scowl.

"What're you thinking, snook?"

"Nothing," he snapped.

At his door, he pushed it wide and moved in. I went after him, since I'd follow my man anywhere, and I closed and locked the door before leaning against it.

Ryo spun around to face me. "I don't understand why *you* would care for *me*."

"Snook—"

He shook his head and waved a hand around. "I don't understand it, *but* I appreciate it, and—" He swallowed thickly. "—I love it."

My body locked.

Did he just say…?

A blush coated his cheeks as he glared and said, "I love *you*."

"Fuckin' Christ. Again, please, snook," I asked as I pushed off the door and stalked toward him.

He backed up until his legs were pressed against the mattress. He tipped his chin up and declared, "I love you."

Cupping each side of his neck, I let out a pleased groan and touched my forehead to his, closing my eyes. "One more time."

"Link—"

"Please, baby. Just one more."

I heard him lick his lips and sigh before he whispered, "I love you."

Opening my eyes, I brushed a thumb over his bottom lip. "Snook, it means the world to me you shared that, and you gotta know I fuckin' love you too. So much."

He jumped at me, lips on mine, demanding and urgent. We wrapped each other up, hands and arms holding each other tightly.

Christ. I needed to have him.

I glided my hands down to cup his arse, gripping. He lifted his legs and hooked them around my waist. I rubbed his hardness against mine, drawing out a groan from both of us.

"Baby, I need you something bad, but we gotta talk first."

He pulled back and glared. Dropping his legs, he stepped off to the side, away from the bed. Dammit.

"I swear, if this is where you're breaking up—"

I launched over to cover his mouth with my hand as I chuckled. "Fuck no, snook. Why would you think that after we just said we loved each other?"

He shrugged, looking away.

Goddamn his family.

Now I really wanted to go find and shoot them.

Gently, I pinched his chin between my thumb and forefinger and drew his hard gaze back to mine.

"I was gonna woo the hell outta you by taking you out to dinner to the same restaurant you gallantly saved me in." He snorted, and his gaze softened as he rolled his eyes. "And I'll still do that, but I gotta share the news now. The news that had me smiling this morning."

He nodded once. "Okay."

I slid my hands to his waist while I quickly glanced around for any weapons. This could go either way, where he'd want to stab me or love me some more.

"Why are you looking around?" he asked.

"In case you stab me after hearing what I have to tell you."

He took a step away and placed his hands on his hips. "Do you have someone pregnant?"

An abrupt laugh escaped me. "What? Fuck no. I've only been with you ungloved."

He dropped his hands. "All right, then. I don't think I'll stab you for anything else." He glanced to his wall where a sword hung on display. "Maybe I should get it." He started to walk off, until, with a chuckle, I wound an arm around his waist and spun him back to me.

"No way, baby."

He tipped his chin up, gaze serious. "Then tell me, please."

Shit. Why was I suddenly nervous?

I shouldn't be. We loved each other.

And it wasn't like he had to move in right away.

I'd give him a week after it was all settled to get his things from here to there.

Actually, he wouldn't even need to move anything in. We could shop together, maybe online so no one spotted him with me. We wouldn't go public about our relationship until he wanted to or asked me to give up the dangerous shit so we could be seen around town.

"Link," Ryo scolded.

"Sorry, lost in thought." I rubbed my sweaty palms up and down my jeans. "Okay. So, great news…." I rushed out the next part. "I bought the house next door, with a thirty-day settlement, so eventually we'll get that secret tunnel done. It'll be safer for us, and we wouldn't waste so much time travelling like we do now, and you could move in when you're ready. But have a think about moving in with me, like I will, when it's all settled." I nodded and then told him in case he didn't get my ramblings, "At the same time as me." To sweeten the deal, I added, "We can buy all the things for the house together. It'll be fun."

His chest rose and fell rapidly as he stared at me with his mouth open and eyes wide.

But when he didn't say anything, I took a step closer to him, hands up and out. "Snook?"

Shit. Was he thinking about getting his sword?

"Baby," I whispered when I stopped in front of him and cupped his cheek with one hand while sliding my other around his waist.

He blinked and snapped his mouth closed before he glared.

I smirked. "Are you thinking about your sword?"

The irritated expression disappeared when he sighed and dropped his forehead to my shoulder.

I wrapped both arms around his waist and ran one hand up his back. "Ryo."

"You're infuriating."

"I know."

His hands gripped my tee at the waist. "However…."

My heart goddamn expanded with hope so fucking fast, I thought it'd crack my ribs. "However?" I pushed.

"You are *my* infuriating boyfriend, and even though I think you're crazy for doing it, I think it's sweet too."

I grinned. "Yeah?"

"Yes, Link."

"So you'll move in with me?"

He blushed. "You would really want me to?"

"For fuckin' sure."

He rolled his eyes and smiled. "At least you have a month to figure out if this is the right choice."

"Baby, I don't need a month. I hate the days I don't get to see you. Need you close, and that house is the closest I can get."

"Normal people would ask their partner to move in with them where they already live."

Chuckling, I kissed his jaw. "I ain't normal. Plus, I can work from anywhere, and I know you want to stay with Wolf."

"I do," he admitted.

"Then this'll work out perfectly, especially when we get that tunnel set up."

He let out a soft laugh. "Link, we don't need a tunnel."

"We don't need it, but I totally fuckin' want one. How cool would it be to sneak back and forth. Then if any shit happens at our place or Wolf's, we can get to safety at each other's. My guards will help Wolf's. It's fuckin' perfect."

His gaze was warm when he softly said, "Our place."

"Yeah, snook. *Ours.* You like the sound of it?"

He licked his lips and then nodded. "I do. But if you change your mind in the month, you let me—" He groaned into my mouth when I took his in a hot kiss.

Licking and sucking down his neck, I told him, "Never gonna change my mind. I'll be like an octopus suctioned to you all the damn time."

"Maybe I do need my sword," he said.

Chuckling, I pulled back. "Uh-uh, snook. You're

officially stuck with me. You told me you love me," I sang.

He groaned. "Dear God, please don't try and sing again."

"But you love me," I cooed.

"If you ever want to be inside me again, you won't do that."

I mimed zipping my lips and picked him up in my arms again. He wrapped around me like a horny little koala.

"Right now, we're gonna move onto the me being inside you part."

He moaned, kissing up and down my neck. "Please."

I took him to the bed and laid him down while I stood back, staring at the man who was mine.

The man I would literally do anything for.

The man I was gonna please for the rest of our lives.

Only one thought sobered me and had me glaring down at him.

His brows pinched. "What is this look for? I'm the one who does that."

"You're not allowed to die before me."

A rough laugh left him. "What?"

"I wouldn't be able to handle it."

"Link, I love you, but right now, we aren't talking about death."

I grinned, and he rolled his eyes at my sudden change. "True, baby, we ain't dampening this moment. You love me, you want me, and you're gonna be moving in with me. Nothing can top this unless you wanna get mar—"

"Link, I swear I will grab my sword if you don't get down here and fuck me."

Smirking, I winked. "Whatever my baby needs, he gets." Man, I couldn't wait until we were living under the same roof together.

YEARS LATER

 yo

THERE WAS a man breathing heavily against the back of my neck. Almost like a chainsaw that needed oiling. Yet, I wouldn't want it any other way.

I love him. Completely and utterly.

He was the first to break down my walls and somehow see I was worthy of his love.

Even when I still let my anxiety rule my actions in public and shut down any moment that made us seem like a couple, Link would just tease me back with a wink or a grin, and later he'd reassure me of his feelings for me.

My stomach fluttered.

I didn't know what I'd done to deserve someone like Link—someone who weathered my moods, distance, and temper and still looked at me like I mattered. Like I was worth loving. It made me feel seen in a way I never had before… and a little terrified of how much that meant to me.

Today, I would prove how much, though.

He would be mine.

I would have *my* ring on *his* finger, so everyone knew he was taken.

And I wasn't only asking him because of the men and women who kept looking at him like they wanted to be in his bed.

Link was mine.

He'd accepted me, flaws and all. I wasn't about to let him slip away or doubt that I wanted a future together.

Slowly, I slipped out of bed and stood beside it, staring down at the naked man. A sheet covered his lower half, but I intimately knew every inch of him.

He mumbled in his sleep and rolled onto his stomach, pulling my pillow down to hug it. His fully inked back was on display.

There wouldn't be a day that went by when I didn't think about how good-looking he was.

How fortunate I was to find the one man who brightened my life with laughs and love.

My heart swelled.

He really was mine, and I would make sure everyone knew. Even when what I would do today would bring my anxiety forward.

For him, I would do this.

With a rush to my pulse, I made my way to the en suite for a shower. I managed to wash my body and hair before a tattooed arm wound around my waist and lips kissed my shoulder.

"Why'd you leave me, snook?"

"You know there are people coming for lunch at Wolf's. I need to check with Katon that everything is running smoothly." Wolf didn't have people coming, I did. I'd reached out to Link's friends and family to come share this moment, and all of them wanted to be here.

My stomach churned.

Still, I knew I could do this.

For him.

He hummed under his breath and pushed his erection against my arse. "Soon, you can go. You sore after last night?"

My body melted against him at the reminder of the couple of rounds we went through. One was slow and sweet, the other hard and rough. Both I loved because they were with Link.

"No, Link. You always take care of me so well."

He turned me and took my mouth in a deep kiss. Lips parted as our tongues slid together in an unhurried dance. Each movement was slow and deliberate, meant to savour rather than rush. It left my head light.

When he pulled away, he dipped back in for a nip and suck to my lower lip as he palmed my hard cock. "You want me to take care of this now or later, snook?"

I wanted him now, but I also had things I needed to do.

I wanted everything perfect.

He grinned and kissed my cheek before he stepped out of the way and tapped my arse cheek. "Go, we'll play later." I stared down at his erection, and he chuckled. "I can wait, too, baby. Besides, you had me seeing enough stars last night, I doubt I have a drop of cum left in me."

"Link." My face warmed.

He chuckled. "You better get going, though, before I change my mind."

I swept close, kissed him quickly, and rushed from the shower to dry.

"Who's Wolf got coming again?"

"People who will bore you."

He snorted. "Baby, I'll sit through anything if I've got you at my side."

This man.

He was the sweetest one I knew.

"You're ridiculous," I told him with a small smile.

He winked. "And you love it."

I did.

"I'll meet you next door later?" I asked, wrapping the towel around my waist.

"You got it, snook. Love ya."

Cheeks warming, I glanced away and then back to whisper, "I love you too." I rushed from the room with a thundering heart over the thought of soon showing him exactly how much he held my heart and soul.

LINK

SINCE I'D BEEN out on business, I kept on my suit for this lunch Ryo wanted me at and walked through the tunnel from our place to Wolf's. Still couldn't believe Wolf had been all for the secret entrance. Though, I think Ruin was the one who talked him into it because he was a lot like me and thought it was cool. Plus, Ryo still worked for Wolf, and it made things a hell'va lot easier getting to and from each other's place.

Up the stairs, I pushed open the door to the new area in the garage that no one was allowed to enter, and I went to the next door. I pressed my thumb against the security panel, waiting for the beep before the door unlocked and I could open it.

No one questioned how I got in the house or what I

was doing there. They were used to seeing me around, and I knew from the years Ryo and I had been together that Wolf's people were just as loyal as mine were, and they were paid well to keep their mouths closed. No doubt they'd have figured out Ryo and I were together.

Ryo still kept any public displays of affection behind closed doors, but anyone could tell I was completely crazy in love with my man.

When I reached the dining room, I pulled the door open and stepped in, then stilled.

"What the fuck?" I breathed, gaze widening.

Trisha was here. My sister and her husband.

Travis, Violet, and Izzy. Bradshaw and some other trusted guards. A few Hawks members, like Talon and Dodge and their families. Then there was Wolf and Ruin.

They'd all turned my way when I'd walked in.

"Ah, I'm not drunk. And I don't do drugs, so is this an intervention about me and Ryo? There's no fuckin' way I'm giving him up."

Some chuckled.

But I was damn serious.

Ryo shifted out from behind Travis, and he looked a little green around the gills.

Had these fuckers said something to him?

"You good?" I asked, walking his way. "Because even though I liked these guys, I'll beat the shit outta them."

Izzy snorted, and there were more chuckles.

But I was goddamn serious.

I ground my teeth together when I realised I was probably fucking up even more by getting everyone's attention on Ryo.

He'd hate that.

"You don't need to hurt anyone," Ryo told me.

Okay. I stopped near him, but not close enough that'd make him uncomfortable in front of people.

"What's going on?" I asked. "Not that it's not good to see you all. Especially you, Trisha." My eyes widened, and I thumbed at Ryo. "Have you met Ryo?" I asked.

Trisha laughed. "I have."

"Link," Ryo said.

I faced him, and when he stepped up to stand in front of me, I grinned. "What's up?"

When he took my hand in his and dropped to one knee, my gut ate my arsehole as my mouth dropped open.

This couldn't be what I thought.

Holy fuck, was it?

"Lincoln Graham, you're the most annoying and craziest man I have ever met, and for some insane reason, you picked me to be at your side." His voice was low and trembled from nerves. "The problem is, I want to stay at your side forever and have other people know you're not available to anyone else but me. So, the best way to do that would be to marry." He drew in a shaky breath. "Will you marry me, Link?"

Jesus Christ.

Jesus motherfucking Christ.

My man had just asked me in front of everyone.

He wanted his ring on my finger. What he didn't know was that I had a ring back in the bedroom at our place and I'd planned to ask him tonight after dinner.

But this was better.

Way better.

"Link?" Ryo said.

"Answer him, dickhead," Travis called.

"Don't call him that," Ryo clipped, glaring over his shoulder.

Travis grinned.

Reaching down, I helped Ryo to his feet and cupped his cheeks.

"Baby, you wanna make an honest man outta me?"

"It's more so other people stop looking at you and thinking you're single when they see no ring."

Laughter sounded.

My grin grew to a crazy happy one. I held my shaking hand out to him as I said, "Snook, I'd be damned honoured to marry you. When? Tonight?"

Ryo smiled as he slid his ring on. The black-and-silver band was one I would've picked for myself. "Not tonight. But soon."

"Got it. We'll do it next week." I leaned in and kissed my man, and for the first time in front of anyone, he pushed against me to kiss me back, wrapping his arms around my neck.

My heart soared.

It was too bad everyone was here, though. I

would've liked to have fucked my man sweet and slow for being brave like this in front of people.

"Let's get this fuckin' party started," Ruin called.

Pulling back, I smiled at Ryo, who returned it.

"Love you, snook."

He wrapped his arms around my waist and kissed my jaw. "I love you, too, Link."

Christ, I fucking knew Ryo and I would have a happy ever after. He was such a sucker for me, but I was glad he was strong enough to let his walls crumble enough to allow me in.

Now he'd never get rid of me.

"What's that smile for?" he asked.

"Just thinking about how you're stuck with me now."

He rolled his eyes and smiled. "I wouldn't want it any other way."

I kissed the tip of his nose. "Me, either, baby."

We were fucking perfect for each other.

Hawks MC: Ballarat Charter

Holding Out: Zara and Talon

Outplayed: Violet and Travis

Climbing Out: Griz and Deanna

Finding Out (novella) Killer and Ivy

Black Out: Blue and Clary

No Way Out: Stoke and Malinda

Coming Out (novella) Julian and Mattie

Out to Find Freedom: Warden and Emmy

Hawks MC: Caroline Springs Charter

The Secrets Out: Josie, Pick, and Billy

Hiding Out: Dodge and Low

Down and Out: Dive and Mena

Living Without: Vicious and Nary

Walkout (novella) Dallas and Melissa

Hear Me Out: Beast and Knife

Break Out (novella) Handle and Della

Fallout: Fang and Poppy

Out of the Blue: Lan, Parker, and Easton

Out Gamed: Nancy and Gamer

Hawks MC: Next Generation

Coyote: Channa and Coyote

Ruin: Wolf and Ruin

Out of Control: Ryo and Link

Texas: Maya and Texas

Swan… I don't want to give it away.

Romania… I can't give this away either.

Diamond MC

Country

State (novella)

Death

Torch

Polished P & P

(MM romances)

Wreck Me Forever

Never A Saint

Working Out West

Up in a Blaze

Romantic Comedies

Fumbled Love

Bumbled Love

Making Changes

Making Sense

Why choose fantasy titles under L. Rose

A Torn Paige

A Lost Paige

A Final Paige

Within the Darkness

Infinite Bond

Protected by the Shifters series

(MM romances)

Protected by the Bear Shifter

Protected by the Tiger Shifter

Protected by the Fox Shifter

www.ingramcontent.com/pod-product-compliance
Lightning Source LLC
Chambersburg PA
CBHW050029040726
47599CB00015B/1595